T

About the Author

Brought up in North London, Libby Patterson studied Politics and Sociology gaining her Degree from Sunderland University. She moved to the Western Isles in 2006 through a work transfer opportunity. She has three grown up children, a son and twin daughters; She now lives in South Uist with her greyhounds and partner.

In 2012 Libby was made redundant and decided it was time to fulfil a lifelong ambition to write a novel. She attended a Crime Writer's Workshop with Caro Ramsay, and that is where Matt MacAulay came to life.

Libby cares passionately about the strength of the community and family values and believes the people of Uist have much to teach the people of wider Scotland and beyond.

About this book

This, the second book in the Matt Macaulay Trilogy finds Matt back in Uist feeling relaxed and happier with life. Now working for the Scottish Security Services he did not expect to be given an assignment quite so close to home; nevertheless he would be working with people he knew in a place that brought back family memories, so didn't anticipate any real problems and was quite looking forward to it. But life isn't that simple for Matt. Odd things start to happen that threaten the very existence of the island way of life. Should he just ignore them and get on with his job? Or is his assignment somehow part of the problem?

Acknowledgements

I would like to thank my friends and neighbours who helped me write this book, adding layers of local colour and authenticity, especially The MacPhee family, Paul Steele, Ken MacDonald, Bryan Learmond, Sarah MacEachen for translating and, Sallyann Cole for copy reading.

Thank you also to my family who inspire me in all that I do.

Also by Libby Patterson:
Hebridean Storm.
Who Said That?

The Uist Connection
Copyright © 2016 Libby Patterson

MATT MACAULAY'S UIST

Sound of Harris

Boneray

North Uist

Lochmaddy

Atlantic Ocean

Little Minch

Baltanich

Benbecula

N

Loch Bee

Loch Skipport

Hecla

BEN CORRADALE

Beinn Mhor

Usinish

Corradale Bay

Sea of the Hebrides

Bornish

Loch Eynort

15 Kms

10 miles

SOUTH UIST

Loch Boisdale

Bryan Learmond © 2016

Eriskay

Sound of Barra

5

Chapter one: Home

The twenty-five miles of soft golden sand that edged the pristine waters of the Atlantic was baking gently in the afternoon sunshine. August days are long in Uist and on this particular Sunday afternoon it was unusually balmy. Despite the fact that all who were able had taken to the shore for the afternoon the sheer expanse of golden sand meant that everyone felt as if the beach, the broad sky and virgin sand was theirs alone.

Across the machair at Bornish the Macaulay family were having a barbeque. Matt Macaulay and his brother in law Iain had built a fire on the beach. They had cheated slightly bringing pre-cooked food from home, but jokingly insisted that it was their skill in heating it up that would be what counted in making it tasty. Kate and Iona, Matt's twin sisters, were paddling in the waves with their friend Marieke and her small son Kazik. The little boy was laughing at being splashed by the family dog, a large black and white greyhound, which was running in and out of the waves, chasing the tide then running away, soaking everyone in his wake. They had met Marieke earlier in the year when Matt had intervened to stop her being mugged, as he thought, outside a bar in Glasgow. It had led to an astonishing pursuit through the Highlands and Islands, which ended up involving the whole family and bonding the two of them as close friends.

Their mother Seonag, with her sister Liz sat in garden chairs close by nursing a small baby, Iona's son Benjamin James, or Benny as he was becoming known. He was nearly six months old and despite his early arrival and small frame, he was a bouncing, lively baby boy.

"I didn't meet her and the bairn, when they were here before, is she all right now?" Liz nodded towards Marieke who was picking up her now dripping child.

"Well, as well as they can be, I suppose," replied Seonag. "The court case is ongoing, but I think she is safe now. They have given them a wee flat; she is hoping to go to college, Matt says."

"That's good, how about Matt? He seems a lot happier now. He's working for that Murdo you said? I thought he was a bit strange, you know."

"Yes, I am so relieved that he has found something that interests him" Seonag looked over at her son. "I was beginning to get a bit worried about him."

"Aye, but what is it that he's doing? Is it safe?"

Seonag creased her brow, as if trying to find the right words. "Well, it's, it's not police work," she paused. "but it's like, hmm, I'm trying to remember the phrase he used." She shifted the baby to her shoulder. Then she remembered, "Discreet government investigations. That's what he said. He's been back and forth to Glasgow. They pay his expenses mind, but I don't think he's done any investigations yet." She smiled to herself, "although I wouldnae ken if he is, he's being that discreet about them as he is about most things." Both women laughed.

Liz looked towards the young men. She was trying to attract their attention to refill her glass. "It won't be dangerous will it?" She asked her sister. "You know, after the last business..."

"I suspect it might be from time to time, you know what Matt's like. He wouldn't be interested if there wasn't some sort of danger in it."

They stopped talking as Matt approached with drinks for them. "Two spritzers, ladies." The six foot marine grinned like a cheeky school boy as he handed them plastic cups containing white wine diluted with sparkling water and a melting lump of ice. "Saving the hard stuff for later are we? Don't want to be drunk in charge of an infant." He teased.

Liz took her cup from him. "Your mam's just been telling me about your new job, it sounds interesting? I take it you'll be working on the mainland quite a bit."

"Aye, probably, back and forth. Short contracts. Can't really see it being here." It will make it easier to see Marieke and Kazik, which will be good too."

"Ohh, so are you and her... Well you know?" Liz raised her eyebrows, wiggled her finger between him and the group now heading back from the water and giving Matt a knowing look.

"What are you two like?" He laughed. "At the moment we are just good friends, she has been through a lot, so I'm not going to be pushing things."

"But some girls like to be chased," chided Liz, "Don't let her slip away."

His aunt did not know the full reasons why Marieke had fled her home country. It would come out at the trial, but he wasn't going to discuss it here. He smiled, shook his head and returned to his fire tending duties.

"What are those Caileachan on about?" asked Iain.

"Watch who you are calling a Caileach young man," chided his mother in law, "I'm not so old yet!"

"They are trying to marry me off!" Laughed Matt.

"Least she's not spending her time telling you how to bring up your bairn. They were telling me I was changing Ben's nappy wrong. When was the last time either of them changed a nappy?"

They were still chuckling as Marieke and Kate arrived. Iona went to check that her son was still ok with her mum. She knew that she had little chance of prising him away from his nan.

"What's so funny?" They were laying out towels to sit on by the fire. Kazik was still running round with the dog. Marieke looked slightly concerned but they assured her that he would be fine.

"Just those two sorting our lives out," replied Iain.

Kate looked quizzical.

"Speculating about what I might be doing," explained Matt.

8

"Making our tea, I hope. I'm starving," said Kate. They served up the barbeque on paper plates, passing round salad and drinks. Kazik happily ate sausages with his fingers, sharing them with his now devoted dog.

"This is good, thank you," smiled Marieke. "Not just food, holiday sunshine, friends." She stretched her arms to include their idyllic setting. I owe you all so much. It is good to be here and be happy now."

"Your English is very good, we will have to teach you Gaelic next," called over Liz. She had not met the girl on her previous visit to the island.

Marieke blushed with pleasure at the compliment. "No, it is a lot better, but not good. I am learning."

"You're staying in Glasgow now?" Seonag half asked and half confirmed for her sister's benefit.

"Yes, before my, err, trouble..." She looked at Matt for confirmation that she was being understood. He nodded. "I wanted to be a teacher, now I think I should try again. I must study English at college, so I will be going to the Glasgow Clyde College. It looks nice, but I don't know how near the river it is. Matt will be taking us when he goes back to Glasgow next. There is even a nursery so Kazik and I can learn together." She fondly tousled the little boy's hair. She looked as pleased as the child did. Matt and Kate shared a knowing smile. She seemed so relaxed and happy, excited about her prospects. So different from the girl they had met earlier in the year. Matt, too, was pleased to see her like this.

Kate was now lying on her towel with a bottle of fruit cider. "And what about you big brother? Are you a government employee again working for that strange man Murdo?"

"Haven't you heard? He's going to be Scotland's answer to James Bond!" quipped Iain.

Seonag sighed, "Don't be daft, Scotland already has a James Bond; Sean Connery."

9

"Isn't that Daniel Craig Scottish too?" Asked Iona, now walking around with her son on her shoulder.

"Nooo," came the group response.

"But he is ginger though," Iain was standing up for his wife.

"No he's not! He's ...what do they call it? Strawberry blonde and he was only in the SAS. I'm proper ginger ... 'African sunset'..." He proudly patted his head... "and I'm a marine. James Bond wouldnae stand a chance!" laughed Matt.

"He hasn't signed up again has he?" Liz leant over to Seonag and whispered.

"No, they say it's a bit like being a priest. Once a Marine always a Marine, or so he says."

Matt was on a roll now, he stood and grinned at his family. "Per mare per terram... Slainte," he raised his bottle.

"By Sea, By Land" translated Kate for his bemused looking aunt. "The Royal Marines' motto."

"Kicks the ass out of Semper Fi!" He raised his drink again.

This time it was the twin sisters who rolled their eyes and exchanged smiles. They were both relieved to have their brother back, even though it did mean you didn't know what was going to happen next. He had taken being medically retired from the Marines hard and it was nice to see him relaxed and laughing again.

Marieke wasn't really keeping up with the conversation, so she busied herself helping Iona with little Ben. Kate took the opportunity to quiz her brother further. She cut straight to the chase. "So how about you and her then?"

Matt shook his head and smiled almost wistfully across the beach. "It's not like that. It can't be, at least not now anyway. She is only beginning to sleep at nights. I pop in to see her when I am in Glasgow and suggested that she spend this few days with us. I think I am more like a big brother to her too." He wasn't telling the whole truth. He didn't really understand what he felt for her and the child. It was just that being with them had helped him to find that piece of himself that had been missing. They made him feel useful again. She had rescued him as much as he had rescued her and that created a bond between them that was unspoken but tangible. He would wait for her.

The new job also made a difference to him. He was now employed as a "Consultant" for Police Scotland. Being an extra pair of eyes or carrying out discreet investigations to help the Police be at their "most efficient". His sisters had poked fun as he had travelled off to Glasgow for work, speculating what he might be up to. In fact, he had not taken on an assignment as yet; it had all been training so far. He had to learn about the law, international relations, Scottish government "Priorities" and of course health and safety. He worked directly to Murdo MacNeil, a man whom he had mysteriously met the previous Christmas while walking in the hills. It was Murdo that had talked him into helping Marieke. On the one hand Murdo gave the impression that it would all be fairly mundane tasks, ground work that the police didn't have the resources to do but there was the something about the way Murdo explained things that gave the impression that he wasn't necessarily telling the whole truth or hinted that there was another aspect that really Matt should get, but he didn't. Nevertheless, it gave him something positive to do that would use his skills and that was what he needed. He would give it a go.

The family chatted as they enjoyed the warm afternoon. They were joined by some friends and a neighbour who brought and played her tin whistle to Kazik's delight. Wrapped up in themselves they did not notice the two men about half a mile away sitting in the dunes. In t-shirts and sun glasses they could have been tourists, but they weren't watching the wild life.

In the midst of the ceilidh, Kate noticed that her sister was sitting slightly apart, watching the children in a detached sort of manner.

"You Ok?" she asked, sitting down next to her on the sand. "This motherhood lark wearing you out?"

"No, she smiled wearily, it's not the motherhood bit at all...more the professional side of me."

"What? You're on maternity leave, they don't want you to go back early, surely?"

"Nothing like that. I am on leave, but my brain is still trained and I am still a specialist in the care of vulnerable children as well as a mum."

"Of course!" Kate wondered where her sister was going with this. Did she want to go back to work?

"It's Kazik, look at him..." She nodded towards the child.

"I thought he seemed fine. Obviously he has been through a lot which makes him a bit clingy towards Matt, but all things considered..."

"No, he's hiding it well. On one hand he is hyper, but when he thinks he isn't being watched he lets the mask slip and is very scared about something. It's not a memory, it's real, there is something very wrong."

It was hard to keep track of time as the sun had no intention of setting until gone midnight, but it was the slight chill on the breeze that told the family that it was probably time to get the children to bed. Packing up their bits and pieces they headed home, to continue the ceilidh at the house. As tea was made and drinks were poured, Liz helped Iona get young Benny settled. Once he was washed and changed she sat with the child on a corner of a small sofa in the kitchen and began to sing a traditional Gaelic lullaby to the infant. It was enchanting and soon brought a hush across the room.

"What is she singing?" whispered Marieke.

"Gille Beag ò, Leanabh Lag ò. It's something about a little shepherd boy," replied Iona.

Young Kazik obviously didn't understand the words, but he didn't need to. While she was singing, he climbed up next to Liz and cuddled in. The child had fallen asleep before the song had ended.

As the lights finally went out in the Macaulay household the two men, now in a grey Vauxhall Vectra made their way out of Bornish onto the main road.

"We could have had them," the passenger said to the driver.

"Maybe, but we were told not to go near the marine."

"He doesn't look that dangerous to me," the first man snorted.

"No, but we can wait."

Chapter two: Glasgow

Matt travelled back with Marieke and her son the following week. She was getting used to travelling and proudly organised her documentation, enjoying her new freedom. They took the morning flight from Benbecula which meant they would be in Glasgow by lunchtime. They had flown back and forth from Glasgow several times over the summer. Marieke insisted on the window seat, she didn't believe she would ever get bored with the magnificent view of the chain of islands and lochs glistening in the sun like jewels scattered on the impossibly turquoise water. She nudged Matt to remind her of the names of the quickly reducing hills as the aircraft climbed.

"It's magical," she sighed.

"Aye," Matt agreed. "When the sun shines." He smiled, quietly pleased that despite everything that had happened to her on the islands, Marieke shared his love for his home.

They took a taxi to her flat, their plan was to drop off the bags, then nip to the shops to get a few things in. The block of flats was run down, neglected and fairly bleak. It was four stories high, built around a courtyard; a type of building common to this area of Glasgow and known locally as a "scheme". As they entered the scheme Matt saw an immediate change in Marieke and her son. She was tense and the child became fractious. Marieke always talked positively about the fact that she had a flat and was safe, but he wondered how long it would be before this place got them down. The walkways stank of urine and worse. Large skip type bins next to the entrance overflowed with smelly domestic waste. Matt didn't want to look too closely at what was littered in the corners of the stairwells, he hadn't been there in a couple of weeks and he was sure it had got worse; he just wanted to get inside. Her flat was on the fourth floor. Kazik was whingeing and muttering something that Matt didn't catch. His mother took him firmly by the arm and talked to him quickly, looking round furtively as she did so.

"What's wrong? Is all this travelling finally getting a bit much for him?" Matt was following behind carrying their bags.

"He will be better inside," Marieke answered as she picked up the child and tried to comfort him. Kazik strained over his mother's shoulder stretching his little arms towards Matt.

"Sorry buddy, we will both be in trouble if I drop your mum's bags." Matt joked, but noticed the desperate look in the child's eyes. Something was bothering him. It was an eerie reminder of when they had first met.

Once inside, they were in a different world. Behind the front door was a short corridor with three doors leading from it. The first, on the left, led to a small bathroom, the next to the living room and lastly, at the end of the hallway a door to the bedroom that mother and son shared. From the living room there was a compact kitchen that faced the main road. At the other end of the room was a large window that looked over the court yard, in front of which was a small sofa. Despite the size it was welcoming and cosy. He admired the way she had worked hard to brighten it up and make it a home. Kate had helped her out, both introducing her to charity shops and giving her furniture and some of the essentials. Homemade cushions and Kazik's drawings pinned up around the walls pulled the decor together to make it comfortable.

As Marieke unpacked her bags in the bedroom Kazik climbed onto the sofa and was peering out of the window. Matt sat down next to him.

"What you looking at bud? Do you want to go out and play?"

Kazik shook his head solemnly. "Mans," he whispered, he was in a world of own.

Matt turned to see what he was watching. It was a concrete play park, with a patch of grass, a bench, a couple of swings and a broken roundabout. Two men were slouched on the bench, a can of something between them, but by the look of them alcohol wasn't their only problem.

"Are the local neds bothering you?" Matt asked as Marieke came back into the room.

She sat down wearily on the only other chair in the room. She didn't need to look from the window.

"No, that is probably Billy and Mo. There is no harm in them. Everyone is nice to us. They say hello and leave us alone. But he..." she gestured distractedly towards her son, "he has it in his head that there is what he calls 'mans' watching us. I look, but I cannot see. I tell him the bad men cannot hurt us now, but he says they are there. He is upset and, well, he keeps going on and it is making me scared too." There was a catch in her voice. "What can I do?"

"Och hen, I wish you had said."

She shrugged in reply. "You are good to us, but what can you do, you cannot stop our bad dreams. I forget when I am in Uist, but here we have to learn to live again."

Matt gently pulled Kazik away from the window onto his lap.

"Silly mummy, hey. You know I won't let any mans get to you, don't you wee man."

The little boy, wide eyed nodded at him slowly.

"Tell you what we are going to do. I'm going to make a couple of phone calls, then we are going to go out and get our messages. We will buy you a big lock for the front door so that you know you will be safe at night. And, if it's alright with mummy, I will stay with you for a few days just to make sure the mans are gone. OK?"

Matt could feel the child physically relax in his arms. He looked over to Marieke who nodded and smiled weakly. "Thank you," she mouthed.

Matt firstly called Murdo and arranged to meet him the following day. He also called home to say he would be staying on a few days. This came as no surprise to his family.

It was a bright, sunny afternoon, the heat wave was holding, although it felt clammier in the city. They agreed to walk to the shops and get a taxi back with their shopping. That way they could get a good look about he told the little boy. He didn't think there was any real danger to them, but he was working on the basis that if he could help Kazik feel safe that would reassure his mother.

A little while later they walked out to the main road, with Kazik on his shoulders Matt took note of the parked cars and the people who were around. A couple of people acknowledged Marieke and gripping tightly onto Matt, Kazik was watching too.

They followed a path alongside a dual carriageway to the shops. The traffic sped by, no one paid them any attention. By the time they got to the shops the little boy was more relaxed.

They did their shopping including a lock with a door chain, a spy hole and the tools to fit them. Marieke made a token protest at the expense and what her landlord might think, but couldn't argue about the peace of mind it would bring them.

That evening they ate pizza and fitted the new locks. Kazik watched Matt work with gravity beyond his years, taking everything in. He insisted on being lifted up to be shown how the spy hole worked. Matt talked to people on the walkway and popped up and down to the corner shop a couple of times. He wanted his presence to be noticed. He didn't say anything, but the car interested him. It was a shabby grey Vauxhall Vectra with two men inside. He had noticed it parked in several different places over the course of the afternoon. He couldn't see either the driver or passenger clearly, probably a drug dealer, but he was sure that they had noted him. There was no harm in letting him know that the young woman and child were not alone. He made a mental note of the registration number V28FJW. Just in case.

The next morning over breakfast Kazik was fretful again, this time though it was over a more normal toddler issue. He had his heart set on chocolate milkshake with his breakfast. His mother said no, but Matt offered to get some from the corner shop. Marieke scowled at him in the same way she had just been looking at her son.

"You are..." she was looking for the word in English.

"Spoiling him, I think you mean, but give me a minute." He sat down next to Kazik.

"Listen to me now bud. You have to be a good boy for mummy when I go out to my work today. If you promise me that you will, I'll go out and check that everything is OK and get you that milkshake." Matt wasn't sure how much he understood, but he nodded back sincerely. Marieke folded her arms, rolled her eyes and smiled. "This is not fair...two boys and only me."

Matt couldn't help himself; he kissed her quickly on the cheek and gave her a friendly cuddle as he headed for the door.

He returned a few minutes later, triumphant with the chocolate drink and declaring that there was no one to worry about outside. He wasn't lying, the Vectra had gone.

They talked about their various activities for the day. Matt was heading off to meet Murdo. Marieke had things to do to prepare for college. He told her that he would be back that evening.

He ordered a taxi into town. As it pulled out onto the dual carriageway his heart missed a beat as he noticed a grey Vectra heading towards them, signalling to turn into the scheme. He considered asking the driver to turn back, but decided that wouldn't help. It was unlikely to have anything to do with Marieke. The best thing to do would be to ask Murdo about it, and get a couple of discreet checks done which would put all their minds at rest.

He met Murdo in the Horseshoe Bar near to the central railway station as arranged. It was an old fashioned pub, a Victorian building that was thronged with travellers. A Glasgow institution, it was deceptively large behind its terraced pavement frontage. Matt knew that Murdo felt the best way not to be noticed was to be very obvious. He enjoyed the anonymity of the crowd. Matt saw Murdo sitting in one of the horseshoe shaped booths. As he sat down he noticed that Murdo had a brown A4 envelope on the table in front of him. Could this be a real job finally? They briefly exchanged pleasantries and Matt told Murdo about Kazik's concerns and about the loitering car. He scribbled the registration number onto a napkin. Murdo took it from him, and folding it neatly he put it in his jacket pocket. Like Matt, Murdo thought it was more than likely to be the local low life.

"Parson and his cronies are all locked up and nobody apart from us knows where she is, do they? Tell her I will get it checked out if it makes her feel better. In the meantime," Murdo pushed the envelope towards Matt. "You read this while I get the food." Matt told Murdo what he wanted to eat and opened the envelope as the Glaswegian walked away.

He took out several sheets of printed A4 paper. Staring at them he was confused. He was confused because he knew exactly what he was looking at, he just didn't understand why. It was an operational order and task description for an international military exercise. As he read on, its' relevance to him became clear although he still didn't quite understand what he was supposed to do.

Murdo returned carrying a large wooden spoon with a number on it. "I saw that and thought of you, as they say." Murdo used the spoon to point at the papers that Matt had put face down on the table. "You know what it is?"

"Yes, although I don't think I was ever on one myself. It's the operational order for a Joint Warrior Exercise. It's a NATO and friends war game that is held in the Minch every year. Although it looks like this one is going to have some of it centred around the rocket Range on South Uist. That should be interesting and I guess that's where I come in."

Murdo nodded. "As you say, these exercises happen every year. They are organised by UK MoD and take place usually in Scotland or Wales. This year it is a 13-day military exercise off the Western Isles, in fact, as you say, at your back door." He pulled up his chair and lent forward. "It's a larger operation this year. There's going to be about thirty warships and submarines, sixty aircraft, and around six thousand personnel from the twelve different nations. Ships, submarines, aircraft and ground troops from the UK, US and other countries are taking part."

Matt was leafing through the papers as Murdo spoke. He stopped as a particular passage caught his eye. "They are going to have authority to challenge local fishing boats, that's going to go down well." He read on further... "GPS jamming may affect fishing boats and ferries' satellite navigation systems...that's going to be popular too."

"Exactly" agreed Murdo. "As part of the ongoing negotiations with our English Neighbours, the question has been asked, *What's in it for us?* here in Scotland. What do we get out of it, and are they really doing what they say they are doing?" What has been proposed is that the Scottish Government is allowed an independent observer to have access to the exercise who will provide a report on a daily basis. Someone who is not part of the military, but understands how they work, but who is also familiar with the terrain so will be best placed to assess any local impact and so that, my boy, is you."

Matt was surprised. Apart from the ongoing argument over Trident, UK military cooperation had never been an issue. "OK, but we have never had a problem with them before. I could list the benefits off the top of my head; they tell everyone what they are going to do. Surely? What do you really want me to do?"

Their food arrived. "I'll get to that," Murdo muttered. Matt moved the papers to one side as Murdo passed him a chunky, hot steak and onion sandwich and a bowl of chips. The aroma reminded Matt of how hungry he was. He took a large bite as Murdo continued.

"To make this work we need to be convincing that Holyrood is really pissed at the UK Ministry of Defence and thinks they are up to no good. The Deputy First Minister has stated that it is only with the inclusion of an independent Scottish observer that we are going to let the exercise go ahead. All the participating countries have agreed to the observer being allowed access. This is a larger exercise than normal and particularly interesting because the Russians have been invited to participate, albeit in a non-combative role. We have argued that we want to monitor what they will be doing in our waters."

Not for the first time Matt noted that the relaxed looking Glaswegian sitting opposite him, dipping a chip in ketchup, really did have friends in high places. "I'd be more worried about the French; everyone is spying on the Russians. So what's the catch?"

Finally, pushing his plate to one side, Murdo cut to the chase. He reached into his pocket and pulled out a folded piece of paper. As he flattened it on the table he explained what he really wanted.

"The post grad school of systems engineering at St. Andrew's University are working on a number of international research projects. Some are secret, some they explained and I didn't understand. The point is over the last few months they have been receiving some very odd emails from a professor, A Anatov from the National University of Science and Technology (MISIS) in Moscow. Now we know this person is a senior government researcher and have seen some papers that have been written in the past, but there is no record of what he is actually working on now. When the University tried to find out they hit a complete brick wall. This was all very curious until his last email, which then made it interesting." He passed Matt the piece of paper.

It read:

Sirs,

Thank you for the information on your project and your invitation. It is most useful to my research. I will be in Scotland as part of the Joint Warrior exercise. If it is possible, it would be most useful to meet then.

Murdo continued, "The thing that makes this really interesting is that the university deny categorically sending anything or inviting any one. They and we would very much like to know what this person is up to."

Matt pondered Murdo's use of the word "we". Matt was being paid through Police Scotland and had told people that was who he was working for, but he had not actually met any policemen to date. With Politicians pulling strings this was taking on a different dimension.

"So what exactly do you want me to do? I can't pretend to be a scientist... that will never work."

"No, firstly, we just want you to make contact. Depending on what they have to say we may want to get them out of there. I am not sure how that will play out, that's for you to find out, but discreetly, that is without letting anyone know until we have to." He tapped his nose knowingly as he spoke.

"But if it's a defence thing surely..." Matt was about to protest, but Murdo cut him short.

"No, it's more an academic thing." If everything is kosher, the university would like to set up an ongoing relationship with him and not have him whisked away to some institution south of the border."

"I see," said Matt. Although he still felt it was a bit dubious, he saw no harm in it really. The professor did contact St. Andrews after all.

22

They discussed the logistics of what would be involved. Contact numbers and protocols. The exercise was due to start in September which was two weeks away. He told Murdo that he would spend the intervening time in Glasgow. Murdo was not overly happy with Matt's ongoing involvement with Marieke.

"If you're going to work for me you can't make life long commitments to everyone you rescue you know, or do I have to make them all ugly old scientists?" He quipped. Matt didn't answer. He knew he was right; he just didn't know what to say.

Matt would be invited by the Range to attend a briefing meeting in due course. Murdo would let him know when it was. Matt was to take it from there. It all seemed reasonably straightforward. It hadn't been mentioned, but Matt wondered if Murdo realised his family had a connection to the Range. It was where his late father used to work. He still knew plenty of people who worked there and who would remember his father, including his cousin Sketch, but he had never been inside its imposing HQ perched on the top of Rueval hill. This could be interesting, he thought: walking in the old man's footsteps.

He got back to the flat about tea time. He and Marieke shared a coffee and relaxed as Kazik watched cartoons. He told Marieke the official story that he would have to go back to Uist to be an observer on the Range for a couple of weeks.

"Nothing dangerous?" She asked sceptically.

"No," he laughed, "Sounds fairly boring."

"Huh, really?" she scoffed.

He changed the subject." I told Murdo about your worries. He says there are drug dealers around here and that is who Kazik may have seen. He is going to have them checked out. Anyway, Parson is in prison and nobody knows where you are, do they?"

"No, well not really."

Matt felt that twinge of uneasiness again. "What do you mean, not really?"

In exchange for her giving evidence against Parson, Marieke had been promised protection. Her flat and her enrolment in college were under a different name. She was receiving a government "allowance", rather than claiming benefits. Apart from Matt and his family, she was invisible. Even his family did not know the full story.

Marieke was staring down at her cup. She spoke quietly.

"I called my mother."

"What did you tell her?"

"Just that we are alive and ok... I didn't want her to worry. I miss her."

"Did you tell her where you are?"

"No, not really, I just said Scotland".

Matt tried to hide his concern. He put his cup on the floor, he was trying to work out the implications of what she had just said. "Scotland" wasn't too bad, but Murdo would not see it that way. Would it really increase the likelihood of her being found from Romania? Would they really come this far? Marieke, talking about it for the first time, was having the same thoughts.

"Have I put us in danger? How would they find me here?" She looked over at Kazik who was still engrossed and continued quietly. "Before I met you, I was running, but I knew what they looked like. Now, I can't run; who do I run from, I don't know what they will look like. Do you know what I mean?"

"Yes," he replied. "But you did meet me and I am going to be here for the next couple of weeks at least. There are a lot of people in Scotland and they don't know what you look like either. Let's not panic. Murdo will check out the local criminals for us. Meanwhile, we both have studying to do, so let's just get on with life and not worry about what probably won't happen."

She agreed, but both of them had lingering doubts.

Matt spent most of the next week helping around the flat, while reading up on the history of Joint Warrior exercises and of the operation of the Range itself. Kazik was pleased to have him about. Marieke said he had stopped having nightmares. She didn't say the same about herself.

Most of his studying was done when the child had gone to bed. They spent several late evenings talking into the night. It helped to talk some of it through with Marieke. She was eager to know about the Uists. The Range had been run by various government bodies, then commercial companies over the years. There had been a couple of unsuccessful attempts to close it as a part of different government defence cuts. Matt explained that when the Range was first opened many islanders had been very suspicious, but over the years as local people were promoted through apprenticeships or came home to management positions; it became a significant part of the local community.

"Some people are always suspicious of the government, especially the military" he explained, "but it brings jobs, which is important. If anything goes wrong in the islands, somebody always finds a way to blame the Range."

"You know a lot about it even before you read," she commented.

"Yes, I suppose. My dad used to work there, you see. It will be good to finally see where dad spent so much of his life."

"You have not spoken of him before. Kate told me that he died suddenly."

Matt usually avoided talking about the subject. Six years later it still hurt, but he wanted to tell her.

"It was very sudden. He was only fifty four. He got up in the middle of the night, we never knew if it was to go to the loo or to get a glass of water, but he never returned to the bedroom. When mum went to look for him he was dead on the landing. When the paramedics arrived they found her nursing him in her arms like an over grown child. We all loved him so much, he was a great dad, but we all carry a pang of guilt with our memories; Mum that she hadn't woken earlier and Kate, Iona and I that we were all away. They told us that the heart attack was so sudden and unexpected that it was unlikely that anyone could have made a difference; I just threw myself into work. The Range has probably changed since dad was there, but I am looking forward to seeing it for myself. I think it will bring back happy memories."

Matt wasn't crying, but looked more vulnerable than she had ever seen him. She instinctively wrapped her arms around him. They held each other tightly, neither wanting to let go. That night Kazik was alone in the bedroom.

The next morning it took Matt a few moments to get his bearings. It was still dark. He was in the flat in Glasgow. The woman cuddled next to him was Marieke. The noise that woke him up was his phone ringing. Who could be calling at this time of the morning? By the time he reached the handset it had stopped ringing, but it flashed accusingly. "Missed call Murdo".

Marieke was still asleep. Matt eased himself off the sofa, he slipped on his jeans and t shirt to head out onto the landing to call Murdo back.

"Did I wake you?" Murdo was expecting Matt's prompt reply.

"No, I just didn't get to the phone on time... Then wanted to step out to give us a bit of privacy."

"Aye right". Agreed Murdo. Matt wasn't sure if he was being sarcastic or not.

"Anyhow," He continued. "We have developments. The exercise is due to start next week and I have finally sorted your introductory meeting with the Range Director for tomorrow, at eleven. OK?" He didn't wait for a reply. "But more interestingly, we have had another communication from the doctor," he hesitated, "or professor, I'm still not sure which he is. Maybe both. I am emailing it to you now." Murdo was uncharacteristically pleased with himself, but Matt was hardly paying attention. He was staring at the grey Vectra, whose two occupants were blatantly staring back at him.

"Aye Murdo, I'll have a look when I come off the phone. I'll read it and come back to you. But afore I do, did you get anywhere looking into that grey Vectra?"

Murdo was slightly put off by Matt's lack of interest, but suspected that he would need to read the email first. He understood what he saw as the need to tie up loose ends.

"Well something and nothing really. Not surprisingly it is a false plate. Belonged to a Ford Focus that met its end several years ago. But there's no record of it linked to any crimes up here, nor are there any new "serious dealers" operating out of Clyde Bank at the moment. So they are probably just run of the mill scum. You have a read of the email, then call me back. I want to confirm the flight and meeting times OK?"

"Aye. I'll speak with you in a bit."

Matt ended the call and switched to his email. The message was certainly more direct and very interesting. It read:

"*Sirs,*

Situation now more urgent. Must make contact."

Matt looked up. The car had gone. He called Murdo back.

"That's short and sweet, d'you think he wants out then?"

"Looks that way. You will need to make contact quickly and if that is what he wants, get out even faster. Can you put plans in place to make that happen?"

"No problem, I can do that." Agreed Matt. He knew exactly who he would talk to; a speedy operation would suit him too.

"Good. I'll get you on the afternoon flight and confirm the meeting with the Range Director tomorrow; let's get this done. I'll send you the details." With his usual brevity, he hung up.

Matt remained on the landing for a further few minutes. There was no sign of the car.

Could it be a figment of his imagination, or had they switched cars? Pull yourself together he

thought, can't let the nightmares of a small child, who did after all have reason to be

suspicious of "mans" dictate what he did. Murdo would keep an eye on her. It would be

fine... but then again...

Kazik was up and Marieke had made coffee by the time he returned.

"Sorry to have disturbed you."

"It's OK, it wasn't you," smiled Marieke. "Was that Murdo?"

"Yes, I'm gonna have to go back to Uist for a few days. I'm leaving this afternoon."

"To observe the military?"

Matt wasn't sure if she was the second person taking the rise out of him that morning.

"Yes, do you want to come?" The words were out before he had a chance to think about

them.

"To observe the military too? I don't think so. Did Murdo mention the car?"

"Yes, he reckoned they are just some local low lifes."

"That is fine then."

"Yes, but I just thought..."

"No, Matt..." she stepped closer to him and put her palm gently on his chest. "No, Kazik

and I have to learn to be strong. Come and see us when you are finished. If I can promise

Kazik that you will be back if he is good that will be a help."

Matt took her hand and squeezed it. "Yes, you know you can." They hugged. She pecked

him lightly on the cheek. "C'mon then time for you to pack up your junk, so I can make my

flat nice again!"

Kazik looked very solemn as he waved good bye. Matt looked forward to the old

familiar buzz of heading into a mission. He wasn't worried as such, he was quietly pleased that there were at least two people, other than his mum awaiting his return. He admired Marieke's attitude to life, he knew it was that strength that had got her through. But he always liked a plan B and resolved to ring Kate and ask her to invite Marieke and her son over for a few days. It wouldn't do any harm for her to have the option to be out of harm's way until he got back.

~~~~~~~~~~~~~~~~~~~~~~~~~~~~

Chapter Three: Work

Officially the Exercise was scheduled for only a couple weeks later, however it was planned for a window of opportunity rather than a specific date to allow for weather and real life operational considerations. As Matt sat in the departure lounge with his phone earpiece in, Murdo filled him in on the background politics.

"You won't believe the international debates that have been going on as to whether you should be allowed to observe or not. It's been great really as it ruffled the feathers of the powers that be in Holyrood, so now they are insistent, even those who did not know why."

By the time he was back home there was an invitation to meet with the Range Director, Mr. Mike Roker in his office in the Range Management Building the following day. The Invitation had the letters RMB added after the building title in brackets. A whole new world of acronyms thought Matt.

Back at home, the one aspect that Matt had not considered was what he was going to wear. Iona had asked him when he showed her the letter. He had told his mother and sister the cover story of his being an observer on the Range, and added that some of the foreign nationals had objected. "You will need to look smart and meeting a Director, representing all of us. You'd better look your best." She chided.

He had been used to attending these sorts of meetings in uniform. "I take it my kilt is out then?" He laughed. The wedding suit would have to do.

The meeting with the director went without a hitch and was easier than Matt anticipated. Just off the main road, ten minutes north of Bornish, the Range Management Building could be found on a side road snaking its way up the steep hillside. As a child he had thought it looked like an abandoned space station nestled into the side of the hills. He was met by an old family friend, Frank MacInnis, who greeted him warmly.

"I've got the job of babysitting you over the next couple of weeks, so you had better behave yourself young man!"

"Och, you know that would be boring now Frank," grinned Matt, "I'm hoping you guys will keep me busy." Matt had always had a quiet admiration for Frank, he couldn't quite remember, but he was sure his dad liked him when he had been a young supervisor. He had a kindly, but intelligent face that inspired trust and confidence.

"We'll see. C'mon. I'll take you to meet the boss."

Matt had to sign in at the reception desk. He was allocated a small locker where he was to leave his mobile phone and any personal IT equipment when he entered the building. He was not surprised, but he played his part and acted as if he was not impressed. "I was going to take notes on my tablet." He protested.

"Them's the rules. We'll give you a notepad and pen," shrugged Frank. He had heard all this before and didn't really see Matt as a big note taker.

The building from the outside looked like a drab industrial box; with no obvious windows and large radar domes dominating the frontage, reducing what little light there might be inside. From the road Matt had often thought that it looked like something out of an old science fiction movie. Once "swiped in" and through the tinted automatic security door he had entered a different world.

Matt followed Frank past a set of stairs along a softly lit, slightly narrow, corridor with large light frosted glass doors at various points along the right hand wall. The sunshine from the office windows shone in through the doors, providing patches of natural light. The carpet was light blue and plush underfoot. The left hand wall was decorated with panoramic scenes of missile firings. Matt would have liked to have stopped and looked at them but Frank was marching on.

"We are going to the boss's office, which is just down here on the right. I know it all looks the same. But think of it as a large square grid, with a couple of bits off the side just to confuse people. There are fire doors at each corner of the square. The various offices and engineering rooms are as indicated by each door. They are all swipe card access. We will let you know where you can and can't get into. On this floor the conference room is at the centre of the grid; while upstairs the control room is in the middle. I'll show you round properly, once we have met Mike. Ahead, one of the sliding doors was open. Inside the Director's Secretary stood up to welcome them in. Matt knew her by sight, but didn't know her well. Nevertheless, she was keen to reassure him that if he needed anything, or if he got lost, (as everyone did to start with), she would be of assistance. "Not much happens here without me being able to sort it out," she laughed. She knocked on an inner door, said a few words, then opened it wide for them. "Come in, Come in, Come in!" Boomed a jovial voice, "You are very welcome."

A tall well built man, in his fifties, with fine blonde wavy hair that sat neatly on his collar. A little longer than it would have been in dad's day Matt thought. He had a wide face with high cheekbones. He had the strut of a man who knew he was in charge as he strode towards them holding out his arms in greeting. His hairstyle and suit were expensive, but possibly designed for a younger man. A company man with aspirations. They shook hands. Behind him was a large desk with a laptop on it. Behind the desk was a large LCD screen that was showing an image of waves. In the corner was a small coffee table surrounded by four easy chairs.

"Let's take a seat while Marion brings the coffee shall we?"

Matt liked the fact Mike wasted no time in cutting right to the chase. He wasn't sure yet if he would like anything else about him.

"I have been intrigued to meet the man that our dear friends in government are so keen should witness my operation. Tell me, exactly what is it that you expect to find?" He had a hint of a Northern Irish accent. Matt got the impression that he was not man to be messed with, or at least that was how he saw himself.

"I hope I don't disappoint," replied Matt. He smiled back. The Director leaned back, making himself comfortable. Frank smiled encouragingly at Matt. It was time to talk himself in. He had a government ticket that would get him through the door, but the more they believed in him, the easier it would be.

"To be perfectly frank," he smiled sheepishly at his old friend, "sorry, no pun intended." Frank rolled his eyes feigning amusement. "To be honest, I should say, I expect to find everything as it should be. It's just that with these post referendum negotiations and just the political times we are living through; I just need to be seen to have done so." The two older men nodded in agreement.

"As to why me, well, you will have seen my CV and understand that I do have very relevant experience, which makes me qualified not to judge you, but the effectiveness of this type of training for the UK and indeed the Scottish soldier. This isn't about what you are doing, but what they are getting out of it. That the UK MoD is not just selling us off as an international playground to make some bucks to pay for the Tory spending cuts." Mike's eyebrows rose at Matt's directness. He hoped that he hadn't gone too far. Perhaps he was sounding too like his sister now. He shrugged his shoulders as if unconcerned, "I hope to show how effective live firing training can be and to lay that and any other ghosts to rest." Despite the fact the Rocket Range was the largest in Europe, there was a perennial debate as to its future and the government's commitment to maintain its capability. Matt wanted to position himself as their ally. He continued. "And my other qualification, courtesy of Frank here, my father and your various predecessors, is that being local, I grew up with you guys being here, I understand the impact that you have locally, both good and bad; so can give an authoritative view on the economic impact and opportunities you provide." Looking slowly at each man in turn, Matt hoped he had said enough.

"Well, I was only sent a summary of your CV, but most people here assure me that you are viewed as somewhat of a local hero."

Mike, weighing up his response, was equally direct. "I didn't know your father, but I do know that he is remembered with fondness, so I am content that you will be able to fit in without disrupting my team." Matt tried to suppress a wry smile. He hasn't asked the right people about me, he thought. But that didn't matter, there were smiles all around.

Behind them a light flashed on Mike's desk. Glancing at his watch he got to his feet. "I am afraid that's my next appointment. It was never in my gift to refuse you access, but I'm glad we have had the chance to meet. I am satisfied that you know what you are about and will be an asset here." He shook Matt's hand; the meeting was over. "Feel free to call in if you need anything. Frank will take you through all the paperwork, I'm afraid there is quite a bit of it, but I am sure you will be used to most of it." The three men headed towards the door.

Frank led Matt back along the brightly lit corridor into a smaller office. As the door slid open, it was like entering another world. They stepped from the clinical, space-age environment to an old fashioned, Victorian den. The office was crammed with a cluttered desk piled high with papers, reports and books. To get to his desk Frank had to squeeze past a filing cabinet that was also piled high with books and precariously balanced folders. Frank nodded towards a seat in the corner, inviting Matt to pull it over. Then hesitated, "Ah just put those...ehm, tell you what... give them to me." Matt picked up a couple of buff coloured files and handed them over.

"Bet you know where everything is." He couldn't help himself and was glad when Frank didn't take offence.

"It's my security system, nobody could take anything from here, they couldn't possibly find it." They laughed. "Some of this is for you anyway." Frank waved an envelope.

There were numerous forms to go through and sign. Procedures and protocols, safety briefs to read, none of it was new to Matt, he felt almost jealous of the guys and girls who were going to be on the ships, he would rather have been out there. The exercise kicked off the following Monday with an 08.00 briefing meeting, where the day's activities would be confirmed dependent on any weather conditions that could affect the exercise and the serviceability of all the ships, aircraft and equipment involved. Matt had done it before for real and now was seeing it from a different angle, with a different job to do. Frank was taking great joy in explaining who and what would be happening over the next two weeks. Matt was hoping that he wouldn't be there that long.

With boyish enthusiasm Frank outlined the game plan. "This is the first time the Range has been involved in Joint Warrior like this and the biggest exercise we have ever managed. There are six nations involved, seven if you count the Russians, but they aren't really playing as such...." He grinned knowingly at Matt, who was remembering why Frank took a bit of getting used to. "Go on," the younger man encouraged.

"Each navy has a vessel in and around the Minch and East Atlantic. They are split into two teams. We have called them Arsenal and Spurs. Or in Ryder Cup terms Europe versus America and friends. Celtic and Rangers might be a bit too close to home. One team has to fire targets from their ships, you know, ROVS with infra-red, while the other team has to hit them. Simple really, the team with the highest score wins."

"But that's not the point is it?" Asked Matt.

"No, well spotted. The objective is to practise and understand the strengths and weaknesses in international co-operation. In each team one boat has the hardware; one has the intelligence and the third the command and control. They have to work together to win. That will be the interesting bit. Each team has one or two observers who will be here on Range monitoring and representing their nation. The rest of their forces will be at sea.

"Why here and not in the States, or off the south of France or somewhere?" Asked Matt. He had trained on American Ranges before.

"Out there," Frank waved towards the window, "We have the largest area of monitored air space in Europe. That means they will be able to play their war games out of harm's way and we will be able to watch and report on them. We provide the framework, a safety Management role and help them analyse their data. But, as importantly, a little island off the West Coast of Scotland is far more discreet and doesn't raise the political hackles that other places might do."

"So what are the Russians doing?"

"Ah now that's the new and interesting bit. Would you believe me if I said Health and Safety?" Matt raised his eyebrows, he did find that hard to believe.

"Yes that was the American response when we first discussed it. To run the exercise, we need to ensure that we have a clear air space and clear sea space, as in no planes, ships or indeed no large groupings of marine mammals. Our radars can only see so far. They have a hard boundary that they simply cannot see beyond. To keep things going, we have better flexibility if we can contact anyone who looks like they are approaching or operating near to the boundary. We obviously put out advance notices to mariners, but you always get someone on the day and you just can't predict the wildlife. We used to use Nimrod aircraft, before they were scrapped, to patrol the boundaries and warn us if anything was coming our way and to keep boats and planes away, but we obviously can't do that now. For smaller exercises we use the Coast Guard aircraft, but they don't have the endurance or availability for a trial this big. The Joint Warrior Team was working with the Russians on another project when the issue of wide Range surveillance came up. Much to everyone's surprise the Russian scientist offered the use of their new sub. I think even the Kremlin authorities were taken aback and the Yanks were not sure if they wanted to accept, but increasingly it became the best option. The Russian sub has new powerful far ranging radar that can track and make contact with surface vessels and aircraft allegedly at amazing distances. It's done some demonstrations for us in the Caspian Sea which were impressive, so we will have to see how it operates in the Atlantic. It will potentially scare the crap out of any fishing vessel that strays into the exercise area when they are contacted by a Russian unmanned sub." Frank laughed briefly at this, the consequences of the impact had probably been analysed somewhere thought Matt. "Is it going to be operated from a Russian warship?" he asked, he hadn't seen that in the brief.

"No we have built a temporary underwater port for it just out into the Minch. It can only be operated from RMB. The other participants wouldn't have agreed to anything else. It's not here yet. They say that it's in transit, which could mean a number of things. Some still view it as a potential Trojan horse. I will believe it when I see it. We do have a plan B if they don't show, but we will then be looking at a more limited exercise. We, on the Hebrides Range, want this to be a success so that we can be involved again in the future; to that end I see your being here and reporting on us as a good thing. I hope you will show the benefit to the UK and the Island economy as a positive, to help our case to stage it again in future. But we'll see. I've gone on enough. You will get the specifics of the day to day operations at the briefing meetings and that should put it all in perspective for you."

"Perfect." Matt smiled. He started to gather the various sheets of paper together. He had his homework set for the weekend. "Do you have the names of the people who are going to be at the briefing on Monday? It would help me do a little preparation and kick off my paper work."

"I'll see what I can do. I'll make a quick call, then why don't we do a quick tour of the operation here and it should be printed off by the time you are ready to leave. OK?"

"That will be great," agreed Matt. "It will definitely make my life easier, thank you." His intention was to get Murdo to run background checks on all the players. UK MoD had probably done it already, but it was always best to know who else was in the game.

It wasn't so much of a tour, but a brisk walk through. In the centre of the building on the ground floor was the main conference facility. The room was dominated by a large black polished wood table that had what looked like a scarlet lightning bolt inlaid in the middle. It was surrounded by about twenty or so leather chairs that could swivel to face the table or the large smart screen that covered the end wall. A Bank of Communications equipment was on the opposite wall.

"Very nice. You don't expect the place to be this high tech from the outside," commented Matt.

"I know, you wait till you see the control room, it all got done up a couple of years back. I'm still working out how to use half of it." They both laughed as Matt followed Frank up the stairs into the main control room. It was a large, dark, windowless room and must have taken up most of the top floor of the building.

It took a moment to notice the gentle purr of the air-conditioning and the frames of large dark flat screens around the walls. There was a central work station surrounded by smaller desks and screens.

"It doesn't look much when it's all switched off," explained Frank. "The Range Controller sits in the middle like a conductor, or the Fat Controller as some unkind wits sometime call him." He laughed as he walked further into the room. "The various participants are assigned a work station. You will have one set up for you. Then the screens provide live links to the various trial elements such as targets or a boat or missile firing if that's what's going on. They are configured for each trial or exercise design, so the Range controller can see everything that is going on." Matt was quietly impressed. It seemed like something out of a sci-fi film rather than the side of Rueval on Uist. He was interested to see what it would be like when it was all in action.

Driving home, he reflected, after all the years of driving past it, he never thought it would be like that.

~~~~~~~~~~~~~~~~~~~~~

Chapter Four: Game on

The following Monday, Frank's enthusiasm was definitely catching. Matt was up early, preparing his suit in the way he used to prepare his kit in days gone by. Murdo had sent him thorough back ground information on most of the participants, which he had perused over the weekend. He was looking forward to putting faces to the names and matching the interesting little notes some Whitehall civil servant had made about some of them. This was going to be interesting. He had also been considering the best way of making contact with the Russian to find out what he really wanted; perhaps even to defect. If the opportunity didn't arise during the trial, there were a couple of social events planned for participants, which would probably be his best bet. He also needed to find time to see a man about a boat, just in case he couldn't simply put the Russian on the next plane. All this was going through his head as he gathered his papers into a rucksack ready to set off. He wasn't worried; he knew the script and had plans b, c and d in his head, so was happy.

"You sure you don't want to take a briefcase?" asked his mother as she put toast and homemade whisky marmalade on the table for him. He was going to moan about her fussing, but the toast did smell good and he couldn't resist.

"No, this will be fine. Don't want to look too much of the corporate type. I'll never be able to carry it off."

"What do you have to carry off? I thought you're just observing?" His mother never missed much.

"I just don't want to be, you know, too stuffy. I want to be approachable and for people to tell me what they really think, or what is going on."

"You will have no trouble there. You always were able to charm folk. You always had girls, and boys, for that matter, falling over you."

"Mother, what are you saying?" Matt laughed in mock horror. He knew she was right though; he did usually manage to talk people round to his way of thinking. It was what he was banking on for the next couple of days.

"What's mother saying?" The back door had opened. In came a slightly sleepy looking Iona, carrying baby Ben.

"I think she's calling me a tart." He couldn't resist the opportunity to wind his mother up. She didn't take the bait, just raised her eyebrows resignedly at her daughter.

"Anyway, what are you doing here so early? Everything ok?"

"Fine, we were awake, have been since five this morning, so we thought we'd nip over and wish you good luck on your first day." Iona lived in the neighbouring village, while her husband worked away; she often popped into her mum's, treating it as a home from home.

Ben looked very interested in his uncle's toast, leaning towards him. "Not this morning wee man, I can't go to work with baby slobber on my suit. Not on the first day any way." Matt ruffled the child's hair and kissed his sister on the cheek. "Thanks, I do appreciate it. It's been a while since I got a cooked breakfast and a send off on a Monday morning. I think it's going to be fairly mundane really, but good to be getting involved with things again." He hugged his mother too. "I'd better be off." Seonag looked at the clock, it was only eight o clock. "You have time..."

"No he hasn't, you remember his pathological loathing of being late. And Ben and I will have the rest of that toast. Bye...good luck," she grinned.

"Just like getting the best seat, that's all." Matt quipped as he headed for the door. "Laters."

The best seat in the house was exactly what Matt was aiming for. He had noted his seat when he had the tour last week; he wanted to position himself to get a good view of the international arrivals. You could tell a lot about people just by observing how they entered a room, arranged their papers and introduced themselves. Matt believed that first impressions really count, especially when you don't know that you are making them.

He had been given a "non-escorted" pass, so had the same freedom to swipe himself into the building and move around as all the other UK employees. He nodded and smiled at the queue of uniforms and suits waiting to be signed in. Others were obviously keen to get on with it too. Nodding again at a couple of people he knew, Matt made his way to the conference room. Frank and a couple of others were there setting up, the smart screen displaying welcome in several languages over an aerial photograph of the island and surrounding waters. "This is impressive," smiled Matt. I thought it would be all overhead projectors and note pads." He quipped. A tall man with gun grey, thick, cropped hair was directing operations. He was smiling and laughing, but his whole demeanour, sharp eyes and erect stance made him obviously in command. There was a line of people waiting to consult or receive instructions, he despatched them efficiently and reassuringly. He turned round, to see who was talking. "Oh it's you, Macaulay." His stern face broke into a wide grin. "I'll have none of your cheek. We've moved on from cannons and muskets. Good to have you aboard Captain." He moved forward and embraced the younger man. Matt had known Skip MacDonald since he was a boy, he had been a friend of his dad's. He knew him as a fisherman and keen golfer; he had never seen him in his day job before.

"Good to be here Skip. I am looking forward to it."

"Well I know this will be tame after your military exploits, but you should find it interesting."

"No," Matt corrected him, "It's easy for those who don't know, to be flippant and dismiss all this as war games, but it's a big deal and important to all who are taking part. Careers and international reputations are at stake. But most importantly it's giving a taste of combat roles to the boys and girls who could well be sent into unfriendly waters in the not too distant future. It's important."

Skip grinned even more. "I told them you would be fine, you get it. None of us originally wanted the distraction of a government inspector following us around and poking his nose in and asking stupid questions during such an important exercise, but when I found out that it was you, I was more than happy. I told Mike you're virtually family and a local hero too. No problemo and I'm sure you will write us a good report, even if I have to help you with it." Still chuckling he turned away to another couple of people who were now awaiting his attention.

Frank invited Matt to take a seat. "That's our Skip, behind the humour he knows every inch of this operation. It should be in your notes somewhere; he is the Range Manager, responsible for day to day operations. He brings people in and knows everything that is going on and how to make it work. Not sure what the Russians will make of him! He is one of a kind."

Matt agreed. "He's always like that, wins people over with a smile and a joke. I couldn't imagine him being any different, not even at work. The Russians will cope...they will have no choice."

As Matt took his seat and prepared himself to meet the visitors he felt guilty. He hoped that his actions would not disrupt the exercise too much. In a strange sort of way, they did feel like family.

The defence world is like a small club, as the various parties came in and hustled around they were all obviously members. A couple of people nodded and gave small smiles. It was obvious that some were a little uneasy and quizzical about him being there. They were aware that he was the dreaded inspector. He looked down his list of attendees and dossiers and started to match up who was who.

The first to join him sitting opposite at the large conference table were the French delegation. Matt didn't need to check his notes. Two petite men, they were almost a matching pair. Captain Thierry Blanc and Monsieur Pascal Rougement were impeccably neat and organised. Pulling their chairs in, they sat up straight and arranged their pens and papers. Blanc nodded to Matt politely; Rougement grimaced after taking a sip of his coffee. MI5 were convinced he was a spook. The Dutch were far more relaxed. Hans and Peter, both naval officers introduced themselves to everyone, shaking hands and beaming, extolling the virtues of the island and the rocket Range. Neither had been to Scotland before and were looking forward to getting into the hills as much as they were the exercise itself.

Matt couldn't help but smile when the UK naval representatives arrived. He knew who they were before they said a word. Lieutenant Commander Bob Halifax looked like a cross between Captain Birdseye and an old seadog. He was a stocky man with a full bushy beard, and thick dark curly hair. He had bright twinkling blue eyes that took in the whole room at a glance.

"Ahoy shipmates," he laughed as he found his seat. All smiles and bonhomie, but definitely nobody's fool thought Matt.

The various officials, military and diplomats filed in, mingling by the coffee machine, before taking their seats. It was nearly time to start. The anticipatory murmurings of different languages filled the room. Then the Americans arrived. They couldn't be missed. Heads turned towards the door as a pronounced southern drawl and lazy nasal laugh penetrated the atmosphere from the corridor. Captain Hank Stinsen and Sergeant Wally Hoffer entered the room. There was nothing subtle about them. Hoffer reminded Matt of a cartoon character with wide shoulders a large chin and slim hips. The captain looked like an aging beach boy...all comb over and teeth. He smiled broadly saying "Hi," and waving like a would be celebrity. The smile however never reached his eyes, making his greeting somewhat hollow and condescending. He had the air of an overconfident politician, who was convinced that everyone was there simply for his benefit. They fussed around establishing which seats were theirs and asking about the running order and what would be happening next, oblivious to the fact that they were holding everything up. As they finally settled, the Sergeant reminded Matt of someone who wanted to be an old fashioned military rottweiler. The hard image was undermined though, by the fact that when he spoke, the pitch of his voice raised as if every sentence was a question. He looked smug and gangly, not suiting the shaved head. His narrow eyes surveyed the room as if sussing out the enemy. A redneck and proud of it, who looked as if he thought everyone else was stupid including his captain.

Skip stepped forward and cleared his throat. When he had everyone's attention he introduced Mike Roker who was standing beside him. The Director briefly welcomed the guests, he talked of the benefits of international cooperation and the productive educational experience they would all have. When he handed back to Skip to run through the plan and protocols for the next two weeks it was obvious that while the meeting had listened politely to the director, they were eager for Skip to get down to business. Matt never really had time for the political niceties; he was more interested in when the Russians would be arriving to take part in all this international harmony.

When Skip finally stood up to speak he had the room's undivided attention. He started with an apology.

"As some of you may have noticed, we have some late arrivals. Seemingly, our Russian colleagues have had transport problems. They are stuck at Glasgow airport. I don't know what the issues are, but at least they can't blame the weather."

"Perhaps they are having trouble finding the excess luggage charge for getting the ROV on the wee plane." Some bright spark joked.

"Well that's as maybe," conceded Skip, "but I suggest we get on with the business in hand."

Skip went on to take the meeting through the protocols of the exercise. What would be covered in the daily brief, what each military unit would be expected to report. How the exercise would be managed through the control room.

The mood, while professional, was light hearted and slightly jovial. It reminded Matt of a room full of excited school boys. He found it a bit unsettling; he remembered it for real, when the brief was about real blood, bombs and bullets, not environmental protocols and Health and Safety. His thoughts wandered, he wondered what Marieke was doing. Snapping back to reality, he looked around the room. The other odd aspect to the meeting was the lack of women present. There were a couple of female Range staff, but all the international delegates were male. Recalling some of the girls he had worked with, he thought that they would probably be on the ships doing the work. They wouldn't have time for this.

The plan was fairly straightforward. They would meet every morning for a brief at which the Range and the day's participants would declare operational readiness. Then, and only then, would the day's scenario be revealed. Who would be attacking or defending and who would be the day's monitors. The reason the exercise was being held on this remote spot of the north west of Scotland was that is gave them the vast expanse of the East Atlantic to work with, but how and where they would operate from would be determined by the weather, confirming areas that were clear of shipping and a number of environmental issues. The Russian ROV would be a key asset in managing these.

It was agreed to postpone the visit to the control room until the Russians arrived. There was a certain amount of diplomacy surrounding where people were seated and what information was shared with whom. It was felt that it would give off the "wrong message" if that was seen to be decided before their "eastern colleagues" arrived. Matt was sure that it had all probably been decided already, but they had to go through the motions of being inclusive even when practising how to kill each other.

People started to ask questions, confirming timings and protocols. Some were busy taking copious notes, even though they would have received almost all the information in their briefing packs beforehand. The Americans voiced concerns about access and security. Captain Stinsen insisted that he wanted it formally recorded that the Department of Defence had objected to the presence of the Scottish government observer. They did not see why he was needed and what right one region of the United Kingdom had to impose this imposition. He was oblivious to the fact that several eyebrows rose around the room when he referred to Scotland as a region. Matt met his eyes across his room and smiled.

"Just doing my job sir, I cannae see that I will get in yours or anyone else's way." He was surprised at the bluntness of the objection, but had no intention of justifying his presence. He just wanted to show that he was not intimidated either. He wondered what the Captain's real game was.

Stinsen held his gaze. "Now I don't mean any disrespect towards you, son. I understand you have a distinguished service record. It's just that there are certain checks and balances that will have to be put in place to keep my lords and masters happy." His hands were flat on the table; he was looking straight ahead as he spoke. As he intended, he held the full attention of the room.

It was Skip that responded this time, "I thought all this had been resolved. What exactly is it that you want?" He wasn't fooled either. `

Stinsen smiled. "I'm sure we can sort this out. Please do understand that Wally and I are so very pleased to be here. This is my first time in Scotland, or indeed the islands. I have researched Benbecula to find out the history and just to get a better feel for the place... "

47

Hoffer coughed, interrupting his Captain. He shuffled with his papers, his eyes darting round the room, trying to gauge the reaction of the other participants. It seemed to Matt that he was either embarrassed at his boss's gushing or by the fact that he hadn't realised that Benbecula was a separate island five miles up the road. He looked around to see how other people were reacting. They were not amused. The French were muttering to each other. One of their support officers, a slight man in a neat suit who had up until then been inconspicuous, couldn't help but roll his eyes.

Hank continued, "Well, all that aside, and to make sure that everything is kept on track, I have been instructed to give daily, real time reports, to confirm that the Scottish Government are not having any undue influence on the operation or outcome of this exercise. As long as I can do that, and report satisfactorily we can go ahead."

Skip looked at his Director and at Frank. Matt wondered how they felt about the Americans feeling the need to police their operation. They didn't let it show.

"But you have secure comms. Every participating country has been set up with your own communications lines, in your own offices. It's on the agenda that you are going to be shown them this afternoon. Frank's team has been liaising with the DoD and all the other MoD's to set them up to NATO specifications. There haven't been any problems have there, Frank?"

"No Skip," he lent forward in his chair. He looked perturbed, not understanding what the issue was; slightly worried that something had been missed. "I spoke with the US embassy yesterday and they told me they had reviewed the plans and they were content with them. I have an email to confirm. Every participating country has its own office with secure lines and access control as stipulated."

"We are happy with the setup, well, as long as there is a coffee machine, that is. .. " nobody laughed at his attempt to lighten the discussion. "It's the access element we need to work on. When I say real time, I mean US time, when my superiors are at their desks. I am going to need access during the night. Would there be an issue with that?"

This time the nonverbal exchange was between Skip and his Director, Mike. It was obvious that this was something they had not considered. Bob Halifax coughed and caught Mike's eye. The stare said it all. He's telling him to get on with it thought Matt.

Mike stepped up towards the table pulling his jacket down as he stood. "In principle, we can look into that." He looked around the room at his own staff, "we don't normally operate, or have visitors working at night, so there are things we will need to consider like staffing and site security. If indeed we are able to manage it for you, we would have to accommodate any others that would require overnight access. Leave it with me."

Despite the lack of actual commitment, the American seemed content. "I am happy to work with you to see what we can do."

Bob smiled broadly; Matt wondered how much influence he really had. Skip shrugged, not totally convinced. "If nobody has any other issues, now might be a good time to show you where you will be setting up. You have each been assigned a member of our team as your liaison officer who will take you to your offices and be available to help you set up and assist in any way, including how to work the coffee machines, Hank."

To finish off, Skip reminded the meeting that the next morning's operations brief would be at 0800 to kick off the first day of operation. It was to be a tactical run through to practise communications and call signs with the Range before the action proper commenced. It was agreed that it could go ahead with or without the Russians.

The delegates finally dispersed to their various corners of the building. Matt wondered how they had found space for them all. It really didn't look that big from the outside.

"Do I need to inspect my office suite?" he asked Frank with a smile.

"Nope, I am afraid you're sharing with me... we will have the best biscuits though! Do you want to have a look at where the other national bases are?"

"Not today. I think after what the Yanks said I don't want to appear too pushy on the first day. I will have a wander round then write up my notes on this meeting. Shame the Russians didn't make it. Could be interesting tomorrow, if that's how they feel about the Scots I almost feel sorry for the Russians."

Leaving the building Matt squinted in the afternoon sunshine. He had no intentions of writing up notes. He was going to see a man about a boat.

~~~~~~~~~~~~~~

Chapter Five: Changeable Weather

Stretching in the afternoon sun Matt felt relieved as he stepped out of the building. It was a bit claustrophobic inside the control building with all those people. You certainly got a magnificent view of the islands from the north side of Ruaval, but it did bring home how little land and how much water there really was in and around the fragile string of islands. A myriad of lochs glittered in the sun. People needed to respect both the hills and the seas to survive.

Matt felt a bit like a guilty schoolboy by skiving off, but he needed to confirm the other arrangements that he had put in place.

He drove south following the mainly single track road, weaving between the hills and the sea. The mountain tops looked crisp against the clear azure sky. Uist often enjoys an Indian summer and despite it being nearly mid September the daytime at least was still warm. There were still tourists about. He passed a pair on a tandem laden with unfeasibly large saddle bags. They wobbled slightly as they huffed and puffed to defy gravity. Matt smiled; he wouldn't fancy camping tonight, the down side of the clear skies was the crisp nights, but at least they looked well prepared.

Matt drove on, reaching the "two way", heading for Eriskay. He was going to meet up with old school friend, Stuart Steele and his pride and joy The Island Adventurer.

Stuart came from a large fishing family, his brothers, uncles and forefathers had played a major part in the local fishing industry, from the heyday of the herring trade in the early part of the twentieth century through to European fish quotas and the increasing expense and logistical difficulties of working on the periphery of northern Europe. Stuart, still in his mid twenties, had decided to do things a bit differently. It wasn't in his blood to move away from working on the ocean, but he had spotted a different potential. Three years previously he had invested every penny he had in a twelve seat RIB. Equipped for passengers, it had previously been a tour boat on the Thames. It had adapted well to the more robust waters of the Hebrides. Stuart had started by taking visitors on fishing and wildlife trips, the open seating gave passengers often wet, but excitingly close encounters with local dolphins, which proved a hit. The first couple of years had been a bit tricky; there were those who were sure he would fail because they didn't think such a flimsy, exposed vessel would survive. But by his knowledge of the local waters, force of personality and sheer hard work, his boat trips had gone from strength to strength, being seen as one of the "must do" activities on a visit to the islands. People loved his banter, the route descriptions, local history and folklore plus his uncanny ability to find the dolphins and sea eagles. Mixed with the sheer exhilaration of the RIB on the ocean, he had found a winner. He was now in a position to buy a second boat, but had to keep the "old girl" going in the meantime and that meant ongoing maintenance between trips.

As Matt pulled onto the Calmac ferry slipway by Traigh Leis, or Bonnie Prince Charlie's Bay where it was said Prince Charles Edward Stuart first landed in the Hebrides, Matt could only see Stuart's behind and legs as he was leaning right under his boat. It was pulled up out of the water and mounted on a trailer. It was a poignant, historic setting for the mundane chores of everyday life. Matt had suggested that they met "out of the way". He knew what people were like; he didn't want any local speculation as why he was hiring a boat trip when he was supposedly working on the Rocket Range.

"You patching holes under there? I'm not going out in her if she's going to spring a leak."

"You won't be going out in her at all if you're going to be rude, Ma tha, I can tell you that."

Stuart got to his feet. "This would have been easier in Lochboisdale Harbour, but I guess it didn't go too well for you the last time someone overheard one of your daft plans did it? So what we up to this time? I just hope it's legal or you have a good brief."

"Huh, who do you think I am? I gave up being a pirate years ago Stuart boy, unlike some people I know!"

"Really? You want to do a quick dash to the mainland, you don't know when, but it will be at short notice... Last minute dot com, I'm not to tell anyone about it, but will be paid well." He raised his arms in mock horror. They both laughed.

"I just nipped down to check that we are still on. I still don't know when it will be yet. Within the next week I think, they're not here yet, so I haven't been able to sort it out."

Stuart gave him a sideways glance. "You mean this person, man or woman is coming onto Uist and we are going to take them straight off again. Last time I checked, kidnapping is still illegal. Think there's a jail sentence attached too."

Matt leaned against the rock armour of the slipway wall and scratched his head. He trusted Stuart with his life, but still had to be careful what he told him. "Fraid so. We won't be kidnapping, but some other people might not be happy."

He thought for a moment, "D'you know, I dunno if it's a lass or not. I was kinda assuming it will be a man from what I've been told. But would you be happier if it's a leggy blonde?"

Stuart wasn't joking now, he was thinking. "Will we be chased?"

"It's a possibility."

"We need to go in the dark then, or at least bad light. They'll know we are heading for the mainland I take it, but they won't know what route we're taking if they can't see me. I don't need lights to find my way out of here and take a couple of detours, so anyone who isn't local... and I am assuming they are not local... will and this old girl is still pretty nippy." He rubbed the transom of his boat affectionately.

Matt didn't answer. He didn't want to worry his friend by pointing out that the ROV didn't need light either, because surely it wouldn't come to that. His job was to get the scientist away without anyone noticing. A chase or confrontation would be a whole different matter. But he agreed that Stuart's precautions would be sensible and was glad that his friend had his eyes open to at least some of the dangers.

The two men stood and worked out the logistics. The sun was warm on Stuart's back, he stretched feeling suddenly weary. They talked about the timings and routes that they could take, depending on what was going on, the different places Stuart could launch from. "Whenever you want will be perfect," assured Stuart, "And if it is a leggy blonde I might even reduce my fee. Just let me know." Matt hoped it would be that straightforward.

The wind was starting to chill as they finished off, but visibility was still clear, Matt could see Barra and Fudgi and the other little islands in the Sound of Barra. But in the distance a dark mist was beginning to form, there was a storm coming in. Matt helped Stuart secure the boat before heading north. As he drove past the bay the light hit the sand with a golden reddish hue. Matt decided to stop to take a photo to send to Marieke. He could get it printed and enlarged to cheer up that flat he thought. The colours were great and she was interested in local history and the Bonnie Prince after all.

As he drove back up over the causeway onto South Uist large droplets of rain began to hit his windscreen with a heavy squelching sound, they becoming more pronounced as he travelled on. The rain was in for the night. He remembered the two he had seen earlier on their bike. He hoped they had found somewhere to bunk down for the night.

The rain hadn't stopped by the morning; in fact it had got worse. It wasn't cold as such, but a dark leaden slab of cloud was weighing down on the mountains, taking away the light and dampening the Uist magic.

You couldn't see raindrops on Matt's windscreen as he drove up to the Control building, it was more as if some invisible hand was pouring from a watering can over his windscreen. The moisture had condensed into a wet blanket that clung to the car and seeped into every crevice. The very air was even damp to breathe as he got out of the car. There was no view from the hillside today.

The day two kick off meeting started on time, but only lasted fifteen minutes. The rain had stopped play. The Met man was apologetic, almost as if the arrival of the storm front was his fault. It was forecast to improve later in the day, so it was agreed to call an update meeting in the afternoon. Skip didn't hang around, he obviously knew what the forecaster was going to say, so kept the disappointment short and sweet. He told them that he was sure people had a lot to do, so would not waste anyone's time.

"He doesn't want to get into a discussion about the unpredictability of Uist weather," Frank muttered to Matt as his boss left the room. Some were discussing it in detail, others were rushing off to communicate the change in plans to their respective vessels. Matt sat for a moment watching them all. He did feel disappointed. Not because of the weather, after all, you get rain everywhere, but because it had stopped the exercise. So much for realism, a bit of rain didn't stop wars and didn't stop people getting killed. He would mention this, after all, he was meant to be critically observing.

To make up for his sloping off the previous day, Matt took the opportunity to introduce himself to the various participants. Ostensibly gaining an understanding of their roles, experience and expectations, but as importantly managing to slip in questions about the Russians; had they met them previously, did they really expect them to arrive? Unfortunately, he soon realised that he probably knew most about them. Most gave him a polite welcome, but did not give anything away. It was interesting to see the exercise from the different perspectives and identify some of the contradictions and contrasting perceptions. He would be impressed if they did actually make it all happen.

The Americans were less hospitable. They were polite but formal. Matt smiled, shook hands and left them to it. He had to get on with his paper work. It probably wasn't like this for James Bond.

A bit later on Matt popped outside to take a break from his computer screen. The afternoon was wearing on and the cloud was finally lifting. He tried to call Marieke, but there was no reply. He wasn't worried, I shouldn't keep pestering her, he thought.

The briefing was called for sixteen hundred hours. The skies had cleared and the mood had definitely lifted too. There was a buzz of excitement as people shuffled into their seats. The room was crowded to listen to a beaming Skip announce that they had the weather go ahead for next day. So the exercise would, at least from the Range's perspective, definitely start the next morning.

The room was more crowded than previously because of the addition of three new people. The new arrivals were two men in uniform, who sat like rottweilers either side of a striking blonde woman with sharp features and neatly cropped hair. Definitely not NATO, Matt mused. One of them reminded him of Elvis Costello, gangly with dark, thick framed glasses in his thirties. The other who looked more senior, was of bigger build, with a strikingly flat face, small eyes and boxer's nose. He didn't look as if he had a sense of humour. The blonde was talking intently to her colleague avoiding eye contact both with him and the rest of the room. Their body language and demeanour were at odds with the fact that they were on a supposedly "friendly" mission. The men radiated an aura of hostility. While others were offering platitudes, the Americans simply bristled back.

Their concentration was interrupted when Skip formally introduced them to the room. Matt wasn't sure if Skip's joke about being better late than never was understood or appreciated. They smiled politely. One of the men gave a brief response. The blonde kept leafing through the papers on the table in front of her.

Frank explained quickly that they had arrived earlier in the day and had been in meetings with Skip and the technical leaders to go through their role and operations. He was quite excited. He confirmed that the ROV was on Range, but they would only simulate its use for the first couple of days to give him time to approve its safety clearances. It was not needed for the early exercises.

"So which one is which?" Matt asked. Skip's introduction had not been clear as they had all nodded in response. Keeping his head down trying not to let the glint in his eye show, Frank muttered,

"One's called Boris something and the other is Ivan. I am not sure which is which, but the one with the glasses allegedly doesn't speak any English. The blonde is our Dr. Alex would you believe. I have been talking to her on line for months and not known that she is a she; astounding! I can't wait to meet her properly. She is the brains behind Putin's new toy. Here to single handedly restore Russian credibility and rub the yanks noses in it."

A couple of jigsaw pieces fell into place. They hadn't been able to find pictures of the good doctor as they had been looking for a man. Murdo would smile and Stuart would be pleased. He also had his plan of approach and a cover for interest in her. He would chat her up! Maybe it would be a bit like James Bond after all.

Matt had always been able to take things in quickly and could then find himself getting bored by the minutiae of planning. He didn't have the patience for the boffins and the military, sticklers for detail and protocols. It wasn't that he had forgotten, but had preferred to blank this bit out of his memory but this was different. He liked Skip's humorous but blunt management style. He used humour to keep everyone in line and keep things moving along, while still being able to drill down into the in depth of knowledge when needed. The team was impressive; Skip and the international management team had created a whole alternative universe and were busy meshing it into the real world in a way that not even their closest neighbours would notice.

The meeting finally finished at nearly 7 o'clock. They were running late. Skip apologised for the timing and asked them all to try and be prompt for the other traditional military necessity, the Officers Mess Welcome Dinner. It had been originally planned for the previous evening but been delayed until all the visitors had arrived. Matt wondered whose decision that was; Skip's or Mike's, practicality or politics? All armies and indeed navies run on their stomachs as did the world of international espionage and international defence sales. The formal dinners are a must, attendance was compulsory. Frank affirmed Matt's view that it was more of a political rather than military dinner. Local dignitaries had been invited to welcome the international visitors to the islands, so everyone would be on their best behaviour. (Matt took that to mean not getting drunk and saying what they really thought). There would be, of course, a more traditional end of exercise event, Frank explained. Matt felt it would be a shame that he probably wouldn't be there for that. He joked about not knowing what to wear as it was his first Mess dinner as a civilian, but that he was looking forward to it.

Later, after discussion with his mum and sister, he wore his "good" suit. It was the one that he had bought for Iona's wedding. His mother cooed and fussed over him.

"I've always liked you in that. It's just that bit more stylish than your normal grey suited crowd." She started to play with his tie.

Matt stepped back and rearranged his neck wear. "I have been able to get myself dressed and go out myself before you know."

"Yes, why d'you think mum's fussing?" his sister teased him.

He tried to Skype Marieke before he went out, but couldn't connect. Must be the remnants of the bad weather, he thought he wondered if Kate had managed to catch her about the proposed girls' weekend. He had promised his sister a few all expenses paid days at the Centre in Aviemore, if she told Marieke that she had been let down at the last moment and needed someone to go with her. He hoped she would go. Smiling at the mirror, he felt and looked good. Iona asked who was he trying to impress. He didn't mention the good looking Russian professor, but went out with a spring in his step. (Professor or Doctor, he wondered, perhaps she could be both.)

~~~~~~~~~~~

Chapter Six: Dinner

The Officers Mess was a fairly uninspiring nondescript brick building on the edge of what was the old military base on Benbecula. There had been a full time military presence on the island at one time; various army and RAF units had been stationed there since the Second World War. There were several thousand personnel based throughout the islands at their peak. The Headquarters base on Benbecula was well equipped and self sufficient with its own bar, chapel and medical centre which now stood like a white elephant next to the airport. Now used mainly for Cadet and TA camps it was now rather too big for day to day military needs. Matt's briefing pack from the Range noted that hosting international exercises could well give the facilities an extra lease of life so Matt could see why they would be keen to show it off.

He met Frank as arranged in the car park. Entering the building together, they were greeted by an old fashioned oak panelled reception area. Mounted on the wall was a large oil painting of a famous military campaign heavily featuring the Royal Artillery. Matt hoped the Europeans would appreciate the art. Frank led Matt in past a wide staircase lined with a sweeping brass banister. "The officers' accommodation is up there," Frank noted, waving his arm. "Everyone else is further down the camp." They exited the reception area through a large panelled door to the right into a comparatively small room adorned with military plaques. There was a horseshoe shaped bar that was already doing a brisk trade. People were crowded round small tables, their heads together conspiratorially planning their tactics for the days ahead, forging temporary alliances. This wasn't just an exercise to them, national pride was at stake. Seeing Matt looking at the plaques Frank explained that they were gifts from every regiment or unit that had ever been to the Hebrides. Matt couldn't help be impressed as he looked around. Some more ornate plaques were obviously ceremonial and probably valuable while others were just stickers mounted onto wood; heartfelt mementoes from soldiers who had served together. Each had its own story.

To Matt, the Rocket Range had always been there. As kids they used to go and hide in the sand dunes to watch the night firings but like many of his neighbours, he had no real idea of the extent of the activity that took place. When he was serving in the Royal Marines, some people had known of the Range when he told them he was from South Uist, but he had never trained there himself.

Using the cover of admiring the art work he took the opportunity to explore a little further. Not that he really expected anything dramatic to happen, but old habits die hard and he just liked to know the lay of the land. At the far end of the bar there was an arched exit that led to another area. Whilst Frank hustled his way towards the bar to get their drinks, Matt wandered towards the archway, nodding greetings to various tables. Through the arch was a short but wide corridor which opened into an anteroom displaying a large, full, trophy cabinet that gleamed as testament to, if nothing else, hours of loving polishing. On either side of the cabinet were two more oak doors. The one to the right had the legend Conference Room carved on it. He tried the brass handle, it rattled but was locked. He moved over to the one on the left. Just as he placed his hand on the handle it opened suddenly in front of him.

Matt was about to make his apologies, but didn't get that far, instead, he stood and grinned, feeling like a foolish school boy. The petite woman before him had dark, curly, shoulder length hair, tied loosely back as she was obviously at work. She was studying a clipboard. As she looked up, surprised that there was someone blocking her path, her blue eyes sparkled in recognition, she could not help but return his sheepish grin.

"Matt Macaulay, I was hoping that we might get a chance to say hello, but I didn't think you'd come looking for me, I'm flattered."

"Hello Donna, Iona mentioned that you were back, I didn't know that you were working here. How's it going? You are looking great."

Matt and Donna had been at school together; in fact, they had had a short romance at the age of twelve, which ended after three weeks when Matt had to make a choice between the school disco and football training. They had remained friends, but hadn't seen each other in years; she had left the island about the same time as Matt. He heard that she had got married or something, he thought she had a child but he wasn't sure, but it was great to see her.

Donna explained that she had studied Hospitality Management in Glasgow, been married and had a small son. Earlier in the year her husband left, so she decided to come home to be closer to her family. She was pleased to have landed the job as "Mess Manager" as she could use her professional skills, plus living nearby she could walk to work and have her mum as a baby sitter.

"I thought it would be just perfect, but it gets a bit mundane sometimes as the military can be set in their ways, could do with a bit of livening up sometimes... You should know..." she smiled weakly. "We will have to get together for a chat, but I am just about to put up your seating plan for this evening, so I'd better get on."

"That's interesting, can I have a peek?" He was using his best boyish grin now.

Donna didn't mind helping out her old friend, after all, she was pleased to see a friendly face. "Go on then, quick, come through, I am laying it out here." Donna had the table plan, the seating list and the separately printed place names.

"Cheeky blighters," Matt muttered when he saw that he and Frank were placed on a table well out of the way of the senior guests. That wouldn't do. "Shall we liven it up a bit and do a couple of swapsies? They won't notice, and it will make the evening far more interesting?"

"What do you have in mind?"

Matt re-arranged the name cards on the plan hoping that mixing things up a bit could be to his advantage. He moved the Russians, American and French, which resulted in the various pairings being separated and he and Frank now being seated at a table with the Russian scientist. He also separated the local guests, spreading them around the room, to try and make his deliberate changes less obvious. "How about that? A bit more international diversity I think."

It was Donnas' turn to laugh. "Hmmf, I can see what you are up to. You'll get me into trouble but I'll see what I can do."

Matt gave her a quick peck on the cheek as thanks and, blushing, she shooed him away. He slipped back into the bar, not noticing that his return had been noted by the American Sergeant.

As Matt re-joined Frank in the bar the older man was having a good natured, but impassioned debate with a French officer about the merits of the European wines. Matt took his tonic water with ice and lemon, (he was working after all). He could drink in his own time.

It was not long before the deep mellow sound of a gong reverberated through the room calling them to dinner. As people took their places, Matt noticed both Mike and Skip looking around in surprise. The company on the top table was obviously not who they expected to find. Hank, however, was delighted to find himself next to a pretty local historian and when he declared to the room in general that this had made his night, it was clear that no-one was going to be moved.

Not everyone was quite so happy though. Matt had put Boris, one of the Russians, on the top table too, but he didn't seem pleased at the honour. He was seated next to Bob Halifax who immediately began to engage him in conversation.

63

"There's no escape there," Matt thought, feeling almost guilty. The other Russian, Ivan, was sitting next to Frank and appeared positively alarmed. Frank will be nice to him thought Matt, not that he felt the Russian probably deserved any kindness. He was now placed across the table from the scientist with Matt, the Dutch commando and Wally the American Sergeant, between him and his colleague. In the original plan the two Russian officers had been placed on either side of the scientist as they had been in the conference room earlier. She did not look as if she minded, but they seemed unsettled. Matt wondered if they were guarding or protecting her.

Matt smiled broadly and introduced himself. The Dutch officer, Hans, responded cordially and even Wally smiled and made a bit of an effort, but both Russians merely gave curt nods and seemed wary. Matt tried hard to start a conversation with the Russian scientist, but she did not respond. He made a joke about being a civilian working with the military, but she wasn't responding to his usually infallible charm and didn't laugh. Wally just gave him a condescending look. He played with his cutlery feeling frustrated. He could hardly say "So do you want to defect?" or even, "So what did you mean in that last email?" without scaring her off. They sat in silence as the first course was served.

The starter was a medley of Uist seafood. This consisted of a large, hand dived scallop, a langoustine in its shell, cold smoked with cream cheese and a hot smoked salmon mouse, all on a bed of fresh green salad. It looked absolutely scrumptious to Matt; he couldn't wait to dig in, but noticed that his neighbour had not lifted her cutlery and was staring at her plate quizzically.

"Is everything ok?" He asked.

In a quiet voice, but with perfect English she asked him what they were eating. There was a menu on a stand in the middle of the table that she must have seen, so Matt was surprised that an international traveller didn't recognise the seafood. Pointing at his own plate and referring to the menu he identified the specific items.

"Yes, yes, I know that," she interrupted, "But why does that say hot smoked salmon when this is clearly not hot?"

Matt explained that it was a local delicacy and the "hot" referred to the method of smoking, not how it was served. It gave the salmon a lighter more delicate texture and taste. She listened carefully then took a small mouthful. She nodded and seemed to enjoy it. She said something across the table to her colleague encouraging him to try some.

"I am telling Ivan what you said, his English is not very good." Matt made a mental note that the Elvis Costello look alike was called Ivan. She then asked Matt if he was a fisherman as he knew so much about the Salmon.

"No," he replied. This was his opportunity. "I work for the Scottish Government and am here as an observer."

She inclined her head slightly to one side as she listened. "So are you a scientist? Or what is your area of expertise?"

"I have a number of areas of expertise, but for this exercise you should consider me as the Scottish Government contact." Did he see a flicker of interest cross her face? Did her breathing just catch for a second? He wasn't sure, but something told him that he might have made contact. He was wary that the American might have been listening, but he seemed to be deep in conversation with Hans.

The second course was served. It was Chicken stuffed with Haggis in a whisky sauce. This time it was Frank who described what they were eating. He had the table's attention as he explained in detail what the Haggis was. He described the little furry creatures that ran wild in the hills and the problems the game keepers had catching them due to their surprising agility and different sized legs. Matt couldn't help but smile as the guests asked the usual questions. Hans asked if they would be likely to see them.

"Only on higher ground," replied Matt, not wanting to spoil Frank's story. Wally sat open mouthed. Alex asked if this was another local delicacy. He needed to draw her in, not play games. "Yes, in the same way as the Loch Ness Monster is an attraction in the highlands."

"I see," she replied. But Matt didn't think that she did really. However, she then intriguingly added. "Perhaps you could take me to see them in the hills." Their eyes met as he readily agreed. Contact was made.

Matt was sure Ivan couldn't have heard or understood, even if his English was better than he claimed, but he must have seen the body language because he and Alex were abruptly interrupted by him calling something sharply across the table in Russian. Alex replied. Ivan stood up, still talking and nodding towards Boris who was sitting stony faced and silent at the top table. Matt wondered if they had been texting or communicating in some way he hadn't noticed. He would ask later if Frank had noticed anything. Alex turned to him and made her apologies.

"We have to go. We have a lot of work to do to prepare for tomorrow. It is because we arrived so late. I am sorry." With that she stood up and they left.

After watching the Russians leave Wally stretched. Pudding was being served, but he refused it saying that he was far too full to eat any more. He suggested to Hans that they might adjourn to the Bar. The Dutchman hastily ate half of his pudding and the two of them excused themselves.

Frank moved over and sat next to Matt. "Your aftershave or something I said?" He asked. "Dunno," replied Matt. "What do you think they are up to? That was very odd. I'd have been Court Marshalled if I left a Mess Dinner like that when I was serving. Can't see it making them any friends here."

Frank nodded in agreement. He looked as if he was staring into space and absentmindedly playing with the table salt and pepper pots. He was reflecting on what had just happened and was acutely aware that their table was suddenly the centre of attention of the whole room. His quiet escorting duties were not going well.

"No, that certainly wasn't normal behaviour for mess guests, I must say. We are not alone in thinking that; you can see that the boss doesn't look pleased." He nodded over to the head table. Matt wondered if he was referring to Skip or Mike, both were staring directly at them, neither senior manager looking as if they were enjoying themselves.

"What did you say to her?" asked Frank quietly

"Nothing! C'mon Frank. There's more to this than I'm getting. What's going on?

Frank did not reply immediately. Matt let the silence hang. Finally, Frank seemed to be choosing his words carefully.

"Well you have seen the plan, the same as the rest of us. We have done this before. The Range, UK MoD and all the rest of them have always liked their war games. They are usually serious but good natured, even when everyone is really spying on each other." Matt looked surprised. Frank shrugged "... well, not officially, but they obviously were. But this time there's more to it."

Frank fussed with the napkins now. He'll have the table cleared if we're not careful, thought Matt. Frank weighed up what he felt he could say. He then made a decision.

"You know what is meant to be happening and indeed it will. We are good at this, but things are being changed more than usual. The ROV was originally meant to be provided by the yanks and they would be the observers. We are all meant to be making friends again after the recent international issues. We are all meant to be united against ISIS, even the Russians, but it is never that straightforward as every country has its own sympathies and its own vested interests. Anyway, at the last moment the Yanks declared technical problems. The exercise was nearly cancelled until the Russians offered the use of their prototype. It was a real hassle to get it cleared. Mountains of analysis work and NDAs to be signed, but we got there, or just about. We had to put limits on its operation because we just don't really know the risks. The Yanks are pretending to be unimpressed but they really want to know all about it too as it is supposed to be very capable. This is all meant to be a demonstration of international cooperation, but it's really just a game of poker, trying to psych each other out." Frank shook his head. "We will just have to wait and see I guess."

Hank didn't stay long in the bar; he too was eager to prepare for the following day. Wally nursed his drink, watching as the diners slowly dispersed. He was hoping that the dark haired, mess manager would return. She had a mane of unruly curly hair that reminded him of the subjects of a pre-Raphaelite painting. She intrigued him, she looked out of place. He didn't normally meet women like her in his line of work. She was a natural beauty, unlike his wife, he thought. He was also curious about what the Government Rep had been talking to her about, she was surely way out of his league.

As the bar thinned out he spotted her talking to one of the Range bosses. Wally couldn't hear what was being said, but her body language seemed relaxed, so she was probably being thanked for her efforts during the evening. She looked tired but he couldn't help but notice the quiet beauty of her smile as she turned back towards the bar.

"Excuse me ma'am, could I possibly bother you for another drink please?" His drawl had softened and was deep and mellow.

"Yes, of course, what would you like?" The tiredness disappeared as she turned to her customer.

"Have you got local bourbon?"

Donna laughed. "Not quite. We do have a couple of island whiskies, Pot Dubh and Te Beag, would you like to try a dram?"

"Well which would you recommend ma'am?" Wally shrugged off his jacket and leaned forward over the bar to get a closer look at the bottles. He stretched his back as he lazily rolled out his shoulder muscles like a big cat ready to pounce. "I'll have whichever one you think is best." He smiled. Their eyes met for a second. Donna couldn't decide whether he looked vulnerable or wicked, his eyes had a lizard like quality, piercing, but calculating as if he was smiling at a joke she was missing. She poured him his drink. The bar was quiet, there were a few stragglers at the tables, and her staff were clearing up, she had a couple of minutes to chat.

"So where are you from?"

"Ohio ma'am, a long way and very different from here."

Donna laughed, "Please stop calling me ma'am; makes me feel like the queen. They call me Donna."

Wally smiled even wider. "It is my pleasure to meet you Donna, they call me Wally." He held out his hand, she offered hers and they shook hands theatrically. Her hand was tiny in his palm. She felt a pang of disappointment as she noticed his wedding ring. Behave yourself she thought. Fancying two men in one evening is a bit much.

"You sound homesick."

"No, quite the contrary. I love to be away." He sipped his drink. "This is good. Glad we are just doing run throughs tomorrow, I may just have another one."

"I thought it all kicked off tomorrow?"

"It does, but I am with the Russkies. As they were late arriving, we are going to have a run through and set them up. So I have an easier day."

"Do you speak Russian?"

"That information would be classified ma'am. We don't disclose who can speak what. You should just assume everyone understands everything."

"Wow, even Gaelic. That's impressive." They both laughed.

"You'd better teach me some for good measure."

Wally sipped his drink. "I couldn't help but notice you talking with that guy... what's his name? Macaulay? Did he have anything to do with the seating mix up? Or was that just you?"

Donna blushed slightly, she was taken aback. She didn't know why Matt had suggested the moves, but felt strangely loyal to him, despite the fact that he had placed himself next to the good looking Russian. "No, I am not sure how that happened; I will have to explain it to the boss tomorrow and I'm not looking forward to that." She shrugged resignedly to close the topic. "I used to be at school with Matt and his sisters, I haven't seen him in years, just saying hello. Why, were you jealous at his being next to the blonde?" She raised her eyebrows and gave him her best disapproving look.

"No way. I was more than happy to have a better view of a certain waitress. Perhaps you organised that? I just don't trust damn observers, no matter how friendly they are, they don't stop observing. You know what I mean?"

Donna was amused by his unashamed brashness and was enjoying the gentle flirting. She was treating it more as a game, but still felt a little uneasy about his being married, even if his wife was a long way away. She had no intention of anything happening, but she wasn't sure about him.

"Do you have kids?" she asked.

"No, do you?"

"Yes, my son, Jamie, he's only a toddler, but my pride and joy."

"That's nice; I'd love to be a dad one day, but can't really see it at the moment."

Donna noted that he didn't enquire about Jamie's dad. On the contrary he seemed very eager to talk about himself. He drained his glass, pushing it towards her for a refill. As he started to talk she wondered how many girls in how many places he had told his sorry story to. Instead of arrogant he became more vulnerable and sad. What was he looking for?

"The thing is Donna," he continued lifting his fresh drink. "My wife considers herself to be a somebody. Not just any ordinary somebody, but your original VIP. She has money, influence, power. Complete with the trophy military husband and a throng of hangers-on. She likes it better when I am away, then she can brag about my exploits and not have to put up with me. She owns everything, or likes to think she does, even me. I'd love to have kids, but she wouldn't want to share the limelight. I'd love to be a regular guy, regular dad... have a life of my own; but I kinda sold my soul a long time ago..."

"C'mon sailor, stop beefing. I'm sure this pretty girl has heard it all before from every lonely G.I Can you bring him a coffee miss? We'll be over here." Upon the arrival of his senior officer, Wally was up straight and on duty again. He didn't even make eye contact with Donna as he followed his captain to a corner table.

~~~~~~~~~~~~~~~~~~~

Chapter Seven: The Morning After

Matt was up bright and early for the morning brief the next day. He checked his phone for messages from Marieke on his way in, but she had not been in contact. He wasn't worried as such, but did think it was a bit odd. "She must be busy," he thought. Although he did wonder what at. It was a nice thought that she may have made friends at college or among her neighbours, he was sure he would find out soon. Meanwhile there was work to do.

The morning meeting ran smoothly. The Dutch were cheerfully popping pills, laughing about playing hard and working hard. Matt was amused at the concept of the military making sure they had their daily dose of green tea and ginger extract. What is the world coming to? He didn't think it would be quite the same for the three hundred or so sailors on their ship that was at anchor just off South Lochboisdale. Hank and Wally sat steely eyed and unamused. Wally's pupils were like pin holes.

"He didn't have an early night either," thought Matt. When Skip declared that the Range was ready and operational there was a sense of palpable excitement.

When the briefing was complete they made their way to the Control Room shuffling quietly, talking in hushed whispers, nervous as if they were about to enter a different world, which in a way they were.

The control room had been transformed. On their previous visit, it had been a large room with desks and screens. Now the big wall mounted screens provided windows into the various control and operations rooms on the ships and equipment stations. The sound was turned off, leaving the curious spectacle of the various activities as simultaneous silent movies showing the real scale of what was about to commence.

Each participant had a dedicated workstation, set up so that they could share an overview of the whole operation or individually connect with their own ship or team, using an earpiece to hear the sound. The desks would be re-configured at the end of each day with the security and communications settings for the next day's participants. As the official government observer Matt had a general clearance and access to most of the operation's communications network.

Skip sat with Frank on one side and a woman assistant on the other at a central control desk. There was a panel of large clock faces above their heads showing the times in various time zones. The desk in front of them housed a built in control panel and screens, with three different coloured phones at one end. Matt made a mental note to ask who they were connected to. He doubted if one went to Holyrood.

Skip was like a cross between a high priest and an orchestral conductor producing a dynamic rock opera in space and time out in the east Atlantic Ocean. Sometimes he was in close conversation with his colleagues, sometimes he stood, waving his arms and giving instructions to the various desks to move vessels or clear a target launch. He was switching between screens ships and "country desks" of the participating nations, giving permissions to fire and manoeuvre to allow the exercise to run smoothly. He was obviously in his element, doing what he did best. Drones were flying, rockets and targets were being fired and people were getting animated. The various desks rapidly gave instructions to their ships, whilst waiting for Skip's blessing for their next move. It was high adrenalin stuff and taken very seriously.

While the room was otherwise focussed, Matt took the opportunity to switch his screen to the ROV Operations room to get a better understanding how the Russians and Americans were getting on. As they were not operational that day, there was no sound, only a picture feed from the ROV control room. In the silence their body language spoke volumes.

Wally and a young lad that Matt vaguely recognised were sitting in front of monitors, obviously intent on what they were doing. Matt looked at his notes; an up and coming electronics apprentice from the Range staff had been assigned to support the international

ROV team. Wearing overalls that had probably never looked so smart, he looked the part. Smiling and attentive, he was obviously pleased to have such an important role to play in the scheme of things. Alex was standing behind them. It looked as if she was trying to give instructions but being ignored, her body tense. She made clipped gestures. It looked as if Wally was doing things but being corrected by the young man and Alex. That fitted in with what Matt had expected to see, but he was intrigued as to what the others in the room were doing. Matt could only really see the backs of the other Russian Officers, Ivan and Boris. From behind, he still wasn't sure which was which, but they were not involved in the technical discussion. Their heads were close together, their shoulders talked; they were tense yet slouched as if bored or generally irritated. They exuded indifference. Every now and again one looked up giving a sideways scowl at the Americans. They either did not appreciate or care that they were being filmed.

Hank, the senior American officer, got out of his chair at his work station and picked up a book that had been left on a side table. He started abstractedly leafing through the book, obviously not paying attention. After his bullishness at the previous day's meeting Matt was surprised that he was not more involved. Perhaps he classed Russians as he did Scots and didn't want to communicate with them either. Matt wasn't usually cynical but he had expected Hank to be more hands on. He was intrigued as to what he might be reading. It didn't look very military. Somebody must have spoken to him. He closed the book and pushed it to one side as he looked up to answer. Something was out of place; Matt shook his head and looked again. Why was that book there? He recognised the cover from somewhere but he couldn't place it. He played with the screen and found that he could zoom in and enlarge the picture. The book became full size on his screen. He surreptitiously moved the cursor. A satisfied smile crossed his face as he zoomed in to enlarge the cover. "I'm good," he muttered to himself as he thought he was almost there. He had to blow it up quite a bit, to get the title, it was just nosiness really, but it was bugging him. He was sure that it was a book he knew. He was sure that he recognised it, from school, perhaps. He sat back, trying to remember what it was when he was interrupted by a loud cough and tap on the shoulder.

He was so caught up in what he was doing that he hadn't noticed Frank come up behind him and look at his screen.

"What are you like...You can't do that!" Matt was taken aback. Frank was pointing at the screen. His voiced had raised several octaves. Almost squeaky! "You will cause an international incident!"

Matt was confused. He looked at the screen again. He had enlarged a section of the screen that included the book and the desk. Since he had looked last Alex had moved into frame and leant over the desk... It looked like he was enlarging a shot of her backside. Franks' exclamation had caught several people's attention. Several necks were craned, as a stifled chortle spread around the room. Bob Halifax was not laughing; he simply raised his eyebrows and shook his head. Oh dear, thought Matt, that's going to grow arms and legs. By the time the story is told the next day, people will be saying that he spent the whole day ogling her. But then again, at least it was a connection.

The day carried on without further incident, in fact it went so well it seemed the exercise might complete early. To meet environmental legislation, the Ministry of Defence had a specific rocket allocation for each day. Once it had been reached the exercise was obliged to finish the firing element for the day. This was a bit of a disappointment as the weather the next morning didn't look good since there was poor visibility forecast.

People started to pack up around him and he looked back to his screen, they were also doing the same in the ROV Operations room. Matt knew he had to act to maintain his contact with the Russian, to keep the ball rolling and now was his chance to do so. The best way not to be noticed was to do things in plain sight, so he grabbed his jacket and made his move. He headed for reception, relying on the fact that the story of his zooming in on the Russian Scientist's behind would have spread before him.

He was right; the guard on reception had difficulty hiding his conspiratorial smirk as Matt approached. Matt played this to his advantage. He explained that he wanted to apologise to the Russian doctor about the misunderstanding. He was keen to get that bit in, but wanted to do it without the embarrassment of talking to her in front of her colleagues. He asked if the guard could delay them somehow when they came to hand their passes in, so that he could talk to the professor in the car park. The guard took pity on him and agreed, leaving Matt to hang about outside, pretending to talk on his mobile, as people started to leave.

It seemed an age before people eventually trickled out. Some nodded as they passed him. A few were going back to their offices while others rushed off happy to get the chance of an unexpectedly early finish.

The Americans came out early. Matt had an urge to ask about the book, but didn't want to get entangled in a protracted conversation; he needed to be ready to pounce. Finally, the Russian Doctor came out alone. She looked behind briefly as if expecting her colleagues to be following her. She paused as if momentarily confused. Matt stepped forward and started to stride towards her.

"Dr. Anatov," he called. She looked towards him, her brow still creased with concern. "Think quickly" Matt told himself. "Don't lose her now."

To his relief, he realised she was waiting for him, although she looked serious, slightly distracted and nervous. He moved in and spoke quickly.

"Hi, hmm, we probably don't have much time here before your friends join us. You can tell them I am apologising for looking at your bottom."

She looked more confused and slightly agitated. Matt pushed gamely on.

"Thing is, I wanted to know, do you want to meet to talk about, I don't know…possibly going somewhere?"

He still didn't know how to say, "Do you want to defect?"

Alex reached forward lightly taking hold of his jacket and spoke quickly into his ear. "Listen, no time for talk now. I need to go, leave, soon. I will run out of time if the exercise finishes early."

She paused and looked him straight in the face. Very close. "You are my contact?"

Matt nodded. "When do you want to go?"

She breathed out heavily as if releasing a lifetime's worth of tension. She closed her eyes, not letting go of his jacket. "You have everything organised?"

Matt was slightly put out that she had to ask. "I have a plan in place. A boat. I just need to know when. We will only need a couple of hours notice for the boat."

"Ok, dawn tomorrow or maybe the day after. I run every night after dinner and in the morning at first light. I like running into dawn. They…" she nodded towards the door, "are lazy and only come out and watch from a distance. They do not run with me. You could pick me up." She thought for a moment. "Watch my route tonight and then we go in the morning. You can see a good place and then I will be ready. OK?"

Behind her the building door flew open. The two frustrated looking Russians stormed out. Alex either had eyes in the back of her head or just sensed her countrymen. She took a step back, slapped his face hard, "Now stay away from me you creep!" she turned on her heel and stalked off towards to her colleagues gesticulating and obviously cursing him in Russian. They sneered at Matt as they led her to the car.

There was a wrap-up brief planned for five pm. Matt knew he ought to attend for appearances sake, but he really could have done without it. He had things to do. He got into his car and drove a little way north to a camping spot by Loch Bi. He parked up and using the phone provided by Murdo, called his employer. He was quietly pleased with himself. He reported that he had made contact and just needed to arrange a pick up a point. The dour Glaswegian wasn't quite so impressed. They still didn't know why she wanted to defect and what she had to offer. That would influence the kind of reception Murdo would arrange for her. Matt explained that he was hindered finding that out with the two minders ever present. They discussed what Matt would do if the Russians followed them. Murdo was adamant that there was to be no bloodshed at a NATO event. Matt agreed that he would only know if it was feasible after tonight's reccie. He explained that if he got enough of a head start and Stuart had the boat ready they should be OK. Matt knew the roads, while the Russians didn't. Murdo wasn't overly convinced, but it all depended on how much they wanted to keep her. Murdo was concerned that they did not know how much support the two Russian minders would have. He did not it want it to get messy. Murdo instructed that if Matt decided to go ahead, it should be done as soon as possible. Murdo agreed at least in principle to have a car waiting in the vicinity of Mallaig pier on the other side of the Minch. "Don't be too over enthusiastic," thought Matt wryly.

Matt made a second call, to Stuart. His friend listened intently. "Is this going to be dangerous?"

"Could be." Matt ran through the possible scenarios in his head. He decided not to mention the possibility that their potential pursuers could have air support. "Need to meet you somewhere easy to get to quickly so we can head to Mallaig as soon as possible." They agreed details. It was forecast to be foggy in the morning which would be an advantage. They agreed on Lochboisdale to Mallaig. Matt wondered if he could make it on to Glasgow afterwards, so tried to call Marieke again. When Marieke still didn't answer he decided not to chase after her. He didn't want to appear too desperate.

Matt was pleased that the briefing meeting was fairly short lived. They confirmed the number of missiles fired and that all the participants' objectives had been met so far. Skip and Frank were pleased and optimistic. They were sure that the fog forecast for the morning would clear for a lunchtime start. That suited Matt's plans. He and Alex wouldn't be missed by the trial team until after they were on the mainland at least. He might even get Murdo to ring the Director to explain. He felt a bit guilty about mucking it all up for them.

Matt went home to have a bite to eat. His sister Iona had beaten him home to tell their mum the gossip about Matt zooming in on a woman's backside on the Range and her slapping his face in the car park. Iona was having great fun, but while she was laughing along he could see that his mother was not pleased.

"It wasn't what it seemed." He offered weakly.

"Well I hope you can explain it to Marieke," was her terse reply.

His hopes were raised at the mention of her name. "Have you heard from her?" He asked eagerly.

"Kate might have," replied his sister, "Why, you worried I might have mentioned it already?"

"Have we still got copies of any old school books?" he asked...

"Well that's a random way to change the subject."

"No I'm serious, that is what I thought I was looking at, it was on a desk, I recognised the cover and zoomed in on it. The woman's bum then just sort of got in the way." His mother and sister couldn't help but laugh at him.

"Look, it was an accident honest. She is far too skinny for me anyway."

"You didn't tell her that did you?" asked Iona, she wouldn't put it past her brother. "Is that why she slapped you?" They laughed again.

Matt told them he had to go out to Balivanich. He casually dropped into the conversation not to worry if he was not back; in fact, he might be gone for a couple of days. His mother was quizzical, but he was evasive. She knew she would not get any further details out of him. She was used to it. He never used to talk about his work. She had hoped that it would stop since he left the services.

He kissed his mother on the forehead and told her not to worry; he would probably be hanging out with Stuart Steele.

"Well that does it." She laughed, "I wasn't worried, but I am now. You two were always able to get into trouble together... just don't get arrested and for goodness sake stay away from leggy blondes!"

Chapter Eight: Balivanich

It was still daylight as Matt drove north although the sun was low in the sky. Matt never tired of the soft evening colours that brought a special warmth of their own to the islands. The exercise instructions had mentioned that dinner was served at eight every evening, which gave him a good idea of where most people would be. He suspected that Balivanich would be littered with people who would recognise him. Even to those he didn't know, his presence had become a bit of a curiosity and he didn't want to give anyone any cause to notice him so had decided to arrive before the meal ended. Alex hadn't mentioned where she would be running, but there was a circular route favoured by runners and dog walkers that he thought would be a good bet. He needed to position himself so that he could track both the route she took and where her watchers would be stationed.

Matt parked in MacGillivrays's car park. The shop was the island's answer to Debenhams. It was set back off the main road, just on the north edge of town. The spot gave Matt an unobstructed view of the entrance of the Mess building and the main road leading to and from it. Conveniently, their delivery van was parked outside, which provided Matt with an ideal screen that hid him from sight from the direction of the Mess.

It was a good spot. A little along to his left was the entrance to the officer's Mess. The gateway was flooded in Security lighting which would give him a clear view of anyone leaving. On the corner of the road opposite was the post office junction from which the road led down past the beach to the airport then circled round through the back of what used to be the old RAF base called East Camp. The old military facility stood as a huddle of disconsolate concrete huts, a remnant of the cold war. They sprawled along the path which meandered back to meet the main road, slightly to the right of where Matt was hidden. He was fairly sure that he would be able to watch someone all the way around. There were a number of distinctive identification points. The oddly shaped drop-in centre, the air-raid shelter that had been converted into curious looking small business units and the large building and parade ground that had been taken over by the community stables. The track weaved its way through, back past him, to return to the village. Now he had just to sit and wait.

Darkness brought the mist and a drop in temperature. Any would be athletes had disappeared. Several people had gone in and out of the Mess. Some stood outside having a crafty cigarette. One couple looked like they were having a furtive romantic assignation behind a corner of the building. Finally, just after ten, Alex and her two colleagues emerged into the gloom. The scientist was easy to spot in her high visibility jacket. She wore it over leggings and some sort of vest top. She was obviously serious about her sport. In contrast Boris and Ivan were huddled in anoraks, their collars up against the damp and hands stuffed in their pockets. They were not intending to go very far, thought Matt. Alex did some stretching then started to run. She headed straight towards Matt. For a horrible moment he thought they might follow her, but thankfully they were not that thorough or perhaps just thought she would be in no danger on this little quiet island. Normally they would have been right. Boris stood by the Mess gate watching as Ivan went towards the car park. Alex ran past. They didn't acknowledge each other. He didn't even know if she had seen him; she was intent on her running. Boris watched for a couple of minutes until till she turned off the main thoroughfare onto the stables road. Ivan meanwhile had brought their car to the main gate, Boris jumped in and to Matt's surprise they drove across towards the post office. Matt wasn't sure what they were up to. A moment later they pulled up next to the Post Office. Ivan turned the car around and parked it facing the airport road. He was positioned so they would see her directly as she emerged from the East camp track. They stayed in the car sheltering from the weather. Alex passed them again in about six minutes. The distance Matt calculated was about a mile and a half. She ran past him five times. The two occupants of the car did not seem to pay her any attention at all. Alex finally stopped at the Mess gate. She was leaning over breathing and stretching. She checked her watch or some sort of pedometer. As she was doing this, her colleagues drove back in and after a few minutes Alex re-entered the building. Ivan and Boris stayed outside a little longer. It appeared one of them was on the phone for a couple of minutes, then they talked together animatedly before going inside. Matt wondered who they were talking to and what they were up to.

Once Matt was sure they were all inside he walked the route himself, taking note of the opportunities available to him. The horses watched him warily as he stood in the shelter of the stables. He didn't notice the onset of the rain; he was weighing up his options.

Back in the bar after dinner, Wally had sought Donna's company again. He had consumed a healthy amount of wine at dinner; he wasn't exactly drunk but just a little excitable and talkative. The staff were beginning to tease Donna that it looked as if he had taken a bit of a shine to her. Feeling a bit uneasy about this, she kept bringing up the subject of his wife and life in the USA. Unused to talking about people other than himself, he seized the opportunity to explain what it was like being a trophy husband and just how good he looked in his dress uniform and that it was his looks that maintained his wife's image. He complained that she did not appreciate him, but boasted that one day he would get his own back.

"Hey, I might even stay right here in Scotland, what do you think?" He leered lustfully at Donna. She was saved by Hank joining them again. He was obviously irritated by Wally's behaviour and apologised for him. Once more he ordered coffees. They drank them quickly and Hank made their excuses as they had work to do. "We have to phone home," laughed Wally, imitating ET. Hank gave an exasperated sigh as they left. Donna looked at her watch and tried to do the maths to work out what time it would be in the states. She wondered who they would be talking to and what they would be saying.

It was nearly midnight when Matt drove home deep in thought. He would be back in a couple of hours but there were things he needed to pick up. When he got home, he headed into an outbuilding and rummaged through an old decorating box and fished out a canister of cavity wall filling spray. He gave it a quick shake and hoped that it would still work and then rummaged further. He was sure there was an old box of fireworks in there.

Instead of going to bed Matt busied himself collecting bits and pieces from around the house. He put the old fireworks in a tin and rummaged around on the coat rack in the utility room until he found an old hoodie and a jacket that belonged to his sister. He spent half an hour crumpling up paper and wood scraps then retrieved some Christmas decorations from the loft. He then packed everything into a rucksack. He crept around in his socks, so as not to wake up his mother. When he was finally finished he collapsed into the rocking chair by the stove and rocked to and fro watching the embers as he contemplated the hours ahead. It had been a while since he had planned a mission. Back then he had a team to talk it through with; he doubted Murdo would be happy if he rang him now. With Marieke everything happened very quickly, this time he was taking the offensive. It should be straightforward, he reassured himself, he just needed to keep his wits about him and stick to the plan. The one thing he didn't fancy was a car chase heading south in the fog, even though he would have the advantage. With any luck they would be well on their way out of Lochboisdale in the RIB before Boris and Ivan missed them. It would be all about timing. He drove back to Balivanich at about four am. Sunrise would be about six, if he could see it in the thickening murk. He did not have time to contemplate the weather; he had things to do.

Matt took the back road north, although longer, it was straighter, quicker. It brought him out a little further north of the town. He pulled over just off the main road. He was a short jog from the stables, but more importantly would have a straight run back to Lochboisdale. He could probably make it back to Stuart in less than half an hour if he needed to. If Boris and

Ivan followed him they would probably take the coast road thinking it was the only road south. He just hoped that his old friend was as good as his word and be able to sail in the fog.

Dressed all in black, Matt shouldered his rucksack and took a gentle jog back towards the stables. Glad to be off the main road, he gently eased open the bolt on the stable door, trying his best not to disturb the horses, yet. As he made his way through the stalls, he talked gently with the large beasts that had turned as one to follow his every move. Their intelligent eyes gleamed eerily in the darkness as he apologised for disturbing them and explained what he was about to do. His calm voice and friendly pat had the desired effect and they allowed him access to place a couple of portable lights in hidden crevices and string some white Christmas tree lights between two pipes. He placed an old transistor radio on the window ledge, hoping that it would still work. He didn't mind what station it played, as long as it made a noise. He wired all the electrics into a timer, setting it for twenty past six. He half hid a high visibility jacket and items of women's clothing in some hay in a stall behind one of the bigger stallions. That should keep them busy he thought. Just to be on the safe side he loosened the bolts on the stalls as he left. "Don't forget I am relying on you guys," he whispered as he left the door just slightly ajar.

Matt picked up the pace as he headed back into town towards the post office. He cut through the old deserted camp rather than going back onto the main road. The sky above the ground fog was a shade lighter; he needed to get there before people started moving about. He still had things to do. He followed the rough track up to the airport buildings, cursing as he failed to dodge potholes and mud. There were no streetlights. Before the post office there was a gravelled road just off to the right which led to the beach and the Coastguard Station. Matt had noticed earlier a metal trailer type contraption parked there that was normally towed behind the Coastguard truck. This could have been weak point in the plan because Matt didn't know how heavy it was and if he would be able to move it. After a bit of grunting and shoving he was able to push it further down the path. He was worried about the scraping

noise it made, the effort made him feel a bit light headed. He was able to get it away from the

building and as near to the grass as he could. He rummaged into his bag and got out the

fireworks, a box of firelighters and the wood chips. He ran some thin cord as far as he could

over a small wall and up onto a grassy knoll behind the post office. Once he was content that

his makeshift distraction had the best chance of working he looked to find himself a sheltered

vantage point. He was able to crouch in the stone back doorway to the post office. He took

the sealant canister and a squidgy carrier bag out of his pack and shrank back into the deep

dark corner. He shivered, the dark and chill combined to make an eerie iciness. Not long

before the fun begins he thought.

It wasn't long before Matt saw the sun creep over the horizon. The mist was a blurred

streak of pink and yellow from somewhere beyond the Isle of Skye. Almost immediately he

saw the slender figure of Alex jogging towards him. As she turned down the airport road a

silver Skoda saloon silently pulled into the parking space it had occupied the previous

evening. Ivan and Boris looked dishevelled; they were obviously unhappy at having to be up

so early. They muttered a few words with each other. This was another risky moment; Matt

needed to get close to the car without being noticed and he wasn't quite sure how. He just

knew he needed to be quick. Suddenly a car door opened, then the other one. He held his

breath, had he been seen? It took him a moment to realise what was happening, he couldn't

believe his luck; they had moved to the front of the car and were passing each other

cigarettes. They hadn't done that the night before, or not that Matt had seen. This was even

better and he seized his opportunity. While their heads were down lighting up their smokes

and keeping low he ran up behind the car and shoved the nozzle of the canister into the

exhaust and sprayed until it was empty. He could hear his own heart pounding, he was sure

they would hear the hiss in the still night, but they were now talking loudly in Russian, oblivious to anything else. Job done, he sprinted back behind the building. He didn't know where Alex would be on her circuit, but to take advantage of the Russians being out of the car, he just had to go for it. He lit the fuse cord and watched as the little ember trickled its way along its length. A long moment passed as it went out of sight over the ridged top of the trailer.

"Yes," he hissed as he saw the ember grow and the first firework erupted nosily into the night. He couldn't see them now, but heard the Russians jump out of their skins as they shouted and swore profusely. Seconds later he could hear their footsteps pounding on the gravel lane that led to the rapidly growing inferno. He caught a glimpse of them as he headed back behind the building. They had weapons drawn; so much for no guns, he thought. He was glad he was going in the other direction. As soon as they were out of sight, down the lane, he ran out behind the car and raced along the main road towards the stables.

He ran at full pelt. He had calculated that the first few seconds were the most dangerous, in case they saw him. He had set the incendiary as a distraction. It was loud and bright, but would only last for a minute or so, it would burn out quickly, so he had to be fast, this was his head start. Where was Alex?

As he approached the stonework of the stables entrance, he could see her hi-vis jacket coming around the corner across the field and past the camp entrance. "Perfect", he thought as they met at the stables gate. She slowed, squinting at the commotion in the distance and at the sight of Matt running towards her. She hadn't expected him to be on foot, she was looking round for a car. There was no time to lose.

"Take this off quick." He pulled at her jacket. She went to throw it on the ground. "No, not here," He snatched it and stuffed it inside his own jacket. "C'mon, quick, this way." He pulled her arm to run with him back along the road. She was obviously not happy and confused about this and it was not what she was expecting; but nevertheless she turned to follow him up the road out of the town. She could see lights and hear noises in the stables ahead. Was there someone in there? Did he intend to hide in there? The horses did not seem happy, she could hear neighing and the stamping of hooves. As she looked behind she was sure she could see the glow of torches in the distance.

Victor and Ivan were thoroughly confused, but their hackles were up. The fire went out as quickly as it started. There was no sign of anyone around. They ran back up to the airport road and strained to see Alex; there was no sign of the yellow jacket. Exchanging glances, they ran back to the car and started it, flooring the accelerator. It surged forward, spluttered, then stopped suddenly, neither man had put their seatbelt on and were both thrown forward, bashing themselves against the steering wheel and dashboard. The driver's airbag deployed with a bang, blocking their view and filling the car with a sharp acrid smell. They thought they were under attack. Ivan shouted in pain and frustration as he clutched his ribs, struggling for breath he peered out the windows. Boris, shaking, tried to start the engine again, but although the starter motor turned nothing happened... it was dead. He started hitting the steering wheel in frustration. Ivan pulled at his arm. "Look, look." He was pointing into the thickening dawn mist. They both peered. They could just make out flickering lights. "It's the building at the end... torches?"

"Could be. Do you think she is meeting someone? They said to watch her."

"They are trying hard to keep us away. We had better let them know that it's rude to leave us out."

"Teach them and that stuck up bitch some manners."

They got out of the car and started to run down the road towards the stables.

Matt was sprinting up a slight incline, the scientist lagging behind. "C'mon!" He hissed.

As they headed towards a bend in the road the first glimmers of dawn were making a feeble attempt through the fog. In a momentary glint of light Alex saw the shadow of the car.

She redoubled her efforts and caught up with Matt. They jumped into the car, Matt pushing Alex into the back seat and instructing her to put on the clothes in a bag there. Without a further word they headed south to meet up with Stuart. As they crossed the causeway into South Uist the visibility began to clear. Matt searched the rear view mirror but couldn't see any lights following them. He pressed on to maintain his advantage. The fog was patchy and was quick to return. As they drove further south it hung spookily around the mountainsides.

"You just stay there," thought Matt, "you are my air support." They were taken by surprise when suddenly they realised they were not alone on the road. There were lights heading towards them. The car passed quickly at a wide point in the road. There was no sign of recognition or even a glance from the other vehicle. They obviously didn't want to be seen either. In Uist it is second nature to note and acknowledge cars on the road, locals would know each other's vehicles and would give a nod or a wave to the other driver. Matt was perplexed that he did not recognise this one or its driver; he wondered who else was rushing about so early and what they were up to. Alex was momentarily alarmed, and glad to see the tail lights fade into the distance.

"Ok, so tell me, what is this is all about?" Matt asked.

"You know what it's about, I want to defect." Her voice was raised, so that he could hear, but Matt couldn't help but find her patronising, her tone implied that she had left the word "stupid" off the end of her last sentence. Looking at her in the rear view mirror, he tried again.

"I guessed that," his tone was flat. He could play hard ball too. "I need to know why. To inform my employers what they should do when we reach the mainland."

He now had her full attention. Her lips were pursed as she turned towards him.

"I am a world leading military scientist. My knowledge will be an asset to your government, or any government in the west for that matter." She spoke quickly as the car sped around the curves.

"As I said, why?" Matt repeated.

"Why what?" She retorted.

Matt rolled his eyes, as if talking to a truculent teenager who was being economical with the truth. "You're a world class scientist. You must have the labs, the budget, the prestige and everything that goes with it. You also must know the West isn't as advanced. Why do you want to give it all up, to step back? Be a traitor? Nobody likes traitors."

"The University is not what it claims to be. I tried to tell them, but the directors and the government do not care. It is they who are the traitors, they have betrayed the people and betrayed me. I will not just tell your government; I will tell the world."

Matt was intrigued. He knew he was hitting home and had to push harder.

"So you have to put up with your two goons, Boris and Ivan. Do you think we will let you roam around as you like? Give you a bunch of cash and let you talk to the press and play at whatever you want. What's to stop you sabotaging our work? We have goons too, believe me. And as for the Americans, well you saw what they were like. To get asylum you need a very good reason."

"I have reason." She looked away, avoiding eye contact. Her whole body was rigid; she was concentrating hard on keeping herself together. Matt couldn't decide if she was going to cry or hit him.

"It has to be worth our while, this is going to cause a mountain of trouble." Matt shrugged as if he couldn't care either way.

Alex hadn't expected to have to account for herself this way. It suddenly occurred to her that she was not sure what to expect. She felt vulnerable and alone. She knew this wouldn't be easy. She was used to being in control, enjoying her work and living a privileged life. She had no concerns about politics, corruption or the plight of the poor. She had been proud to be working hard for mother Russia. But then one night, working late, she had made a horrifying discovery. She didn't grasp the scale of the operation at first, and thought it was a rogue scientist. But as she raised the alarm, talking to her seniors, the directors, the education department and even the police, the scale of the operation and cover up became evident. Over recent months she had tried to warn people anonymously. But they knew it was her. Things rapidly went from bad to worse, this was her only chance to save herself, and all those who were in danger. She had no choice. She hadn't planned to tell her story in the middle of a Scottish island to a man she had never met, she didn't know if this man would believe her, but she realised she had little choice.

She leant forward in her seat leaning on the dashboard. She spoke in a flat quiet voice. Matt had to strain to hear.

"I am a woman of thirty years of age. I live in Moscow. My parents died when I was young, I was brought up in an orphanage. Despite my humble beginning, it became obvious that I was going to be a gifted scientist. I worked very hard to get where I am. I cannot say I gave up a lot, as I had nothing to lose until recently. The state gave me everything. At university I became friends with another girl. Very good friends. To put it plainly, I do not like men. Not that way. This is not a way of life my government normally tolerates, but they needed me so they pretended not to see. We had both worked at the university for five years, when I discovered what the Human Science Department was really doing." She paused hugging herself hard, eyes scrunched tight, "I cannot say it here, it is too, too ... I cannot say... ... No!" It took her a minute or two to compose herself before she continued. "They first claimed they did not believe me. It was when I produced evidence and started to warn people that they turned against me. My sexuality became an issue. I was the "disgrace". I was told that I was mentally ill and imagining things and that this was linked to my sexuality. If I wanted to keep my job and position, I had to get better." She snorted in disgust, the pain obviously still raw. "To help me get better I had to marry a man, or else. The state department even had a list of acceptable men and would pay for the wedding. You see I was their... poster girl. The one they had saved. People believed what I had to say. I said no. It didn't take much thought. I had been poor before. It could have been done. But you don't disobey papa Putin. A couple of months ago Olga had an accident... " Alex choked as she said this gripping onto the seat with both hands, her knuckles white. Her slight frame shook. She took deep breaths in an attempt to pull herself together. Matt felt cruel for forcing this out of her; it was obviously still an open angry wound. He suspected too that there was more to come. She took in a deep breath and carried on.

"That is when I met Ivan's senior officer. He told me how exactly the accident happened and what would happen to me if I did not forget what I had discovered and choose a husband from the list. Being poor was a luxury that would not be available to me. Then we had our sea trials for the ROV, I was hoping to escape then, but things did not go well ... there were technical issues. They blamed me for these, I was a subversive. My future had vanished; my accident was only a matter of time." She looked Matt directly in the eyes; he saw her determination and grit. "I offer my brains and my knowledge and the best and worst of the soviet education system, but I have to stop them."

Matt wanted to know what she had discovered, but they were heading into the approach to Lochboisdale Harbour. They swept along the harbour road. It was the end of the season, so there were only a few tourist boats in the water. Thankfully the fishing and fish farm boats had already left for their day's work. Discreetly tied up between the wide slipway and the long quayside was Stuart and the Island Adventurer.

Matt left the car at the further edge, out of sight of the main road. He pulled a bag from the boot and they headed toward the quayside, signalling for Alex to follow. She scanned the pontoons to identify their mode of transport. At first she didn't notice the man beckoning them from the slipway. It was only when Matt began to quicken his pace towards him that she began to take note. He was carrying something that she recognised, but her mind wasn't working properly, she couldn't think of the English word.

It came to her. "Survival suits? Why will we need them?"

Stuart handed her a suit to put on. "I hope this fits. Matt didn't tell me what size you would be." He smiled, but she didn't return the pleasantries.

"But where's the boat?" asked Alex

She was hugging herself tightly against the morning chill. This was not funny. Her heart sunk as the little RIB came into view.

"We are going to Edinburgh in this"?

"C'mon. Let's not hang around." Matt chivvied.

Alex remained on the slipway just staring at the boat. "You are serious. We escape in this." She waved her arms dismissively.

Stuart looked offended.

"It's the quickest and least conspicuous way to get to Mallaig on the mainland," assured Matt. "There will be a car to meet you there and I will come back here for early afternoon, to keep an eye on your colleagues. In the meantime, get on board and make yourself comfortable.... Just do it quickly!"

Alex climbed aboard reluctantly. Stuart didn't waste time, he pulled quickly away as they clambered into the survival gear.

Alex was still not convinced. "But what about this? Is it safe?" She waved her arms again, this time at the all enveloping fog.

"It's good" Matt tried to reassure her. "It will hide us."

The engine purred as they eased out along the sea loch towards the open sea. If they had been heading directly to Mallaig it would have taken just over two hours, but Matt knew it was going to take a bit longer as Stuart had some detours planned.

"It is about to get very noisy" Matt told her. Stuart just wanted the journey over and done with so wasn't wasting any time. They were travelling at fifteen knots with no lights. As the speed increased the engines shrieked and vibrated them to the core. Once they were clear away, he signalled to Stuart to slow down so that he could talk with Alex, she looked as if she needed reassuring.

The Island Adventurer was fitted out with bench seats, each with its own hand rail. Normally people would sit three abreast. Once into her survival suit, Alex had slumped onto the bench in front of Matt, holding on to the rails and looking ahead. As the boat slowed down, Matt tapped her on the shoulder and then moved round to sit next to her. It was still a strain to talk, but at least now it was manageable. He wanted her to finish her story.

"Have you Ear protection?" was her only response.

Stuart shook his head.

"You are going to kill me. I would be safer in Russia." She was clinging onto the rail and did look to have gone several shades paler.

In an attempt to lighten things Matt turned round and called to Stuart in Gaelic. "Do you think I've pulled?"

Stuart laughed back, "Don't you go pestering my passengers now!"

They continued at speed, so Matt decided to leave it to Murdo to get further information out of her. Alex was focussing her body and soul on not being sick and falling apart. In the mist with no visibility there was only the noise of the engines, a sharp reek of diesel and the vibration of the boat. This gave Alex a tense anxious feeling, making her feel as if they were the prey in the vast ocean. Even with his close friend Matt didn't like feeling that much out of control and vulnerable either.

Matt sensed before he actually realised that something was wrong. Neither he nor Alex had noticed that Stuart had slowed the boat right down. Stuart was looking around; listening, and then he leant over the side of the RIB. He cut the engine. It was the sudden silence that drew Matt's attention. "What's up?" He asked. Stuart had made his way to the front of the boat, he leaned over to one side and then the other. He sounded as if he was swearing and praying at the same time. "What is it?" repeated Matt.

"Dunno," replied Stuart. Even in the dim light Matt could see that the blood had drained from his face and his voice was strained.

"Look!" he pointed at the water. "Oh God, man, listen." This time, his voice broke.

Matt listened. Alex looked around. It was completely silent. It was deathly quiet. Matt thought it was the fog at first, but then he followed Stuart's lead and looked over the side of the boat and couldn't quite understand what he was seeing. He looked over to Alex who was leaning over the other side. She turned. She was even paler, her eyes wide. Her expression frozen in confused shock. The water was still and clear, more like a mill pond than an ocean. Suspended in it was a montage of fish, just floating, hanging there, quite still in the water jostling against each other and very dead. There were loads of them, big, small, different shapes and sizes. It would have been a wondrous sight had they not all been dead. The sea was thick with them. Stuart was barely holding it together, he looked as if he was about to cry. Matt had a lump in his throat.

Suddenly, as if a man possessed, Stuart sprang into action. He rummaged round in a store behind the control board and pulled out two buckets,

"C'mon," he thrust a bucket at Matt. "We should at least collect a few to take back to find out what's wrong. We have to do something. Jesus!"

95

Matt looked around. They were alone, possibly the only living beings for miles. There were no birds to be seen, even the damn seaweed was dead. Stuart was right, they had to do something. He grabbed a bucket and passed one to Alex. They all started scooping fish into the boat. "We need to understand what's happened, I'll drop you two and then take the samples to SAMS in Oban."

"Who is Sam?" asked Alex.

"It is a University and centre of aquaculture research," explained Matt. He thought her question was a bit odd, as was her behaviour. She was kneeling on the floor of the boat looking at the fish, holding them up to her face and stroking them gently. The two men looked at her; what she was doing?

"They are not sick, it is not a disease," she said quietly. "Stunned, I think. Some are still alive."

"How could they be stunned?" Stuart was puzzled. "That's daft." The two looked at each other in confusion.

Stuart became suspicious. "It couldn't be what's going on at the rocket Range?" He asked.

"No," they both replied in unison.

"It couldn't be your ROV, it's not been used yet has it?" asked Matt. He was trying to rack his brains for any clue. Alex was picking up the fish gently rubbing them.

"No, not at all." She was a little too quick to reply. The others just stared at her. Matt thought he knew the ROV hadn't even been set up yet, why was she unsure?

"No, I don't think so," she paused and thought. "In the Caspian Sea, the radar was tested, but that was at different configurations and at a far stronger level. It is not the same."

Stuart's whole world was crashing in around him. He came menacingly closer. "I think you need to explain yourself quickly lassie if you want me to take you anywhere."

"No, no, no it couldn't be," she shook her head, still grasping the fish. "There was only an issue in the Caspian Sea trial when the ROV radar was pushed to maximum power, far greater than is being used here. It stunned all the sea life. Most survived, it only lasted a few hours."

Matt and Stuart were slack jawed at her revelation; Matt couldn't quite believe that this was happening. Stuart's brain was flooding with every conspiracy theory that he had ever heard about the Range. Alex tried to reassure them and bring them back to the task in hand.

"But any way, we only got here yesterday morning; it has not been used yet. If it is radar, it must be one of the other ships. Look, I am sorry, but we need to get out of here..." she looked at both men hopefully. "Let's go?"

Stuart finally found his voice, trying to quell the tirade of horrors rushing through his head. "Naw, hang on....are you saying that you have seen this before and it could really be connected to the Range? I was thinking of a disease or something."

"It is a possibility, but nobody should be using radar like that here. Look, they will be fine," she shrugged, "We need to go!" she urged.

The fog was clearing and the crisp morning air penetrated through their survival suits. They were all beginning to feel the cold and were now shocked and angry besides. Alex was used to getting her own way and didn't appreciate the impact the sight of the dead fish was having on the boys. She was becoming increasingly desperate. "We must leave now".

But the two young men couldn't just sail away. This was too important, too fundamental to their way of life.

"Naw, well something's happened," Stuart was still in shock, but not going to be rushed. "I'm not so sure, maybe you didnae do it, but somebody has caused this and you lassie, may be our best bet to sort this out. I'm gonna need to circle round to see the extent of it." He pointed at Alex, "this needs sorting out before I take anyone anywhere."

The boat moved slowly, Stuart filming and taking photos on his phone. He had got over being sad and was now angry. "Whoever has done this is going to pay," he muttered darkly.

"We have to go back" Matt told Alex. She was wide eyed with horror; she couldn't believe what she was hearing.

"No," she pleaded, "Don't go back, I might not get another chance."

"Yes, you will." Matt tried to sound more confident than he felt. He had no idea how Murdo would react to this, but what else could he do?

"Could Ivan or Boris have orders you don't know about to use the ROV to somehow spy on the NATO vessels?"

She shrugged.

"We need to stop them if they are, it's more than just politics or the war games, it's ... it's Uist. If they keep doing this they could destroy our seas, our fish and our way of life... Do you understand?"

She understood but couldn't afford to let compassion for them get in her way. "But we don't know that it is anything to do with our ROV or even anything to do with the exercise or anything else on the Range... they could kill me!"

"I won't let them kill you. But I won't let them kill the islands either. What else could it be? We are going back. Help me at least rule out the exercise and I will get you out of here."

Alex's face was icy. Yet, up close her fury burned in her eyes. She was fuming as Stuart turned the boat back towards Lochboisdale. She couldn't believe she had left herself dependent on such a pair of sentimental.... she couldn't bring herself to call them fools, what would she have done if someone polluted the Kronotsky Zapovednik, how would she react? Matt sat next to her. He seemed calm for somebody who had probably just disobeyed orders. She felt a little more assured as he explained how they would explain her actions. At least he had a plan.

"We will be back in Balivanich by about 10.30. I will drop you off out of town, you walk back in, saying that you saw all the commotion in the stables this morning. You saw Boris's deserted car and got scared and decided to run and hide and have only found your way back now that it is daylight and hopefully safer. Then we go back to the control room as normal at mid day and find out what is going on. OK?"

Alex worried that she would not be believed. Matt secretly agreed with her, but there was nothing he could do now. She had to stick to the story. The fact that she was back should reduce suspicion and be evidence of her "innocence". They may not be convinced, but the absurdity of the situation was actually on their side. They would have to ride it out. He hoped that she was up to it.

~~~~~~

Chapter Nine: What next?

They drove back to Balivanich in silence. The shock of what they had seen and the complications facing them were screaming for attention in Matt's head. Alex's turmoil was the fury of being so near, but now so far from her salvation. She had shared the boys' shock, but it was nothing to do with her. Would she get a second chance? To add insult to injury Matt asked Alex to lie on the floor in the back rather than sit on the seat. He had thought about putting her in the boot, but from her reaction to simply being asked to lie on the floor he was glad that he hadn't. It hadn't been like this last time. He was going to leave her north of Balivanich; she had changed back into her running gear and was going to walk back. He was quite pleased that they had made it as far as Market Stance which was virtually there, without being seen. He hoped that he would be able to claim he had been at home all night and ask what the fuss was. There was a deli and coffee shop on the road just out of the town. As he approached it he passed Donna walking along the road pushing her baby in a pram. She gave him a cheery wave. "Damn, busted," thought Matt. Then he saw an opportunity. He pulled the car over and told Alex that she could sit up. He switched off the engine and waited for Donna to catch up.

"Well hello, fancy seeing you here," she grinned mischievously from ear to ear, leaning in to see Alex who looked dishevelled on the back seat. "Glad the weather is starting to clear; I can't believe I am out walking in the rain. What are you two doing? Out for a run?" She winked.

Matt, winked back, "Something like that, but what are you doing walking in the rain? I'd offer you a lift, but I don't think we'd get that pushchair thing in the boot."

"Och, don't worry. Did you hear about all that commotion at the stables this morning? Don't know what was going on, but it upset the poor horses no end, what a racket. Anyhow, it woke Jamie and he's been bawling ever since. He usually sleeps in the buggy, so this is my desperate attempt to get some peace." She paused and gave Matt a sideways look.

"If you're not offering a lift, why did you stop? I know you, it wasnae just to say hi."

"Aw Donna," He gave his best boyish pleading look. "But since you mention it, we could use a favour?"

"Go on," she was not going to commit herself.

"Thing is, Alex here has to get back to the Mess, but there will be a heap load of trouble if she is seen with me or can't explain where she was earlier. Things really aren't what they seem, honest, but you know what people are like."

Donna looked sceptical. Matt continued, it was always best to stick to one story and he thought it would help to rehearse it for Alex. "I am not really sure what happened, she was out for a run then heard all the noise at the stables too. She couldn't find her colleagues so got a bit of a fright and took off and hid. I picked her up.... No idea where she has been, up near Griminish I think, but she doesn't know. The thing is, it would be far better if people, especially her Russian pals, you know, thought that you picked her up, she is worried sick? She might appreciate some dry togs too, to go back in."

Donna was still sceptical, but she felt sorry for the Russian girl, she did look in a bit of a state.

"Go on then," she agreed. She opened the door for Alex, "Actually, you will be doing me a favour. If you say you were with me, it will stop the gossip about me and that slimy yank. I don't want people thinking he was with me. He really does talk some pish!" Alex got out of the car and shivered against the cold. Donna fished a waterproof out from under the pram. "Put this on, it's Uist so I always carry a spare."

As the two women headed down the road towards town, Matt turned in the Deli car park and headed up south.

Matt was relieved that there was no one in the house when he returned home; he had time to shower and change before heading back to the Range for the twelve o'clock brief. Standing under the hot water he stretched his muscles and twisted his neck trying to relieve the tension in both his mind and body. He was frustrated that he hadn't managed to deliver Alex to safety, but at the same time he shared Stuart's outrage at the murder of innocent animals. Should they have carried on? Murdo would probably think so. It was a dangerous mix and he didn't have much time to resolve either situation.

The mood was completely different on the Range. Most of the guests were smiling, impressed that the Met Officer had been uncannily accurate in that the haar sea mist had cleared leaving a bright clear day. When the Russians arrived, however, they did not seem to share the light hearted mood. Alex was flanked closely by her minders. Matt merely nodded at them as part of his greeting to the general group. They nodded back, though Boris and Ivan were too preoccupied with glaring at the Americans to notice him. Oh well, thought Matt, let them take the flak, happy not to be a suspect.

As the room filled there was gossip and polite condolences offered about the fact that Ivan's car had been vandalised. The Russians thanked people equally courteously, but no mention was made of Alex's mishaps. It was believed to be the same people who tried to break in at the stables. Frank explained in what sounded to Matt like a rehearsed statement, that unfortunately, like everywhere else, Balivanich had its anti-social element, with drink and drug issues. He believed that several people were being questioned. Matt played with his paperwork while Frank gave this explanation. He felt a little sorry for whoever had been picked up, he was sure that Murdo would put it right eventually.

It didn't take long for the meeting to agree the day's objectives and for everyone to slip back into their designated places. Skip did inform the group that there had been reports of some sort of minor environmental incident south of the Range boundaries. It was nothing to do with them and being investigated locally, he had been asked to ensure that no ships operated in that area. Matt's blood ran cold. "Minor!" he wanted to shout, "You should have seen it." There was hardly any reaction to this piece of information; everyone was keen to move on. Matt was slightly annoyed that this appeared less interesting than a damaged car. Who was hiding what, he thought. He didn't want to believe that it could be the Range.

As he took his seat in the control room, Matt noticed Frank and the young member of staff in the ROV room talking in what seemed to be an animated fashion. On the screen both the Americans and Russians were watching unsympathetically. The four men were like a set of bookends, with hard looks and their arms folded across their chests. Alex, on the other hand was listening intently. She glanced towards the camera a couple of times. A cursor flashed on the main control panel. The Intercom system crackled into life in the control room with the brief message. "Delay in ROV launch. Estimated time to launch now plus fifteen minutes." Matt was dying to know what was going on.

His phone vibrated in his pocket. He looked around guiltily to check that nobody had noticed. He had forgotten to hand it in. Skip had reprimanded someone the previous morning about having a phone in the building, he didn't want the same embarrassment, so couldn't answer it. He decided to nip out in case it was Stuart and maybe try and bump into Frank at the same time.

Outside, standing on the edge of the car park, in the bright but cool air, Matt stood with his back to the wind as he returned Stuart's call. He could have sat in his car, but the clear air and moving around was helping his thought processes. He listened intently as his friend, sounding increasingly bemused, described how the effect seemed to be "wearing off". He wasn't really sure what Stuart meant, it had all looked very grim, how could the wee fishes be swimming round normally now? Stuart had been in contact with the Harbour Master, but by the time they went out again in the RIB there was nothing to be seen. He was frustrated that he couldn't mention Matt as a witness. The Harbour Master would report it to the Council Environmental Officer in Stornoway. There were some remaining dead fish, but not on the same scale as earlier. It was being treated as an isolated incident as it only happened in one place. The authorities didn't think it could have something to do with the exercise as it was outside the Range operational boundaries and if a toxin had been the cause, it would have been more wide spread. They couldn't work it out.

"I think they think I'm a daftie making it up," moaned Stuart. Matt agreed to check all the ships movements' logs, to make sure they were all where they were meant to be. "If it's all OK, can we think about taking Alex out again?" Matt ventured.

"Maybe." replied Stuart tentatively. "But you watch them... this observer thing is for real now, Ma tha."

His mind was buzzing as he turned back towards the Control Building. Just before the entrance his phone rang again. It was Murdo and he was not happy. Matt had left a message earlier saying that the plan had to be aborted, but now had to explain himself. He decided to take this call in the car.

Murdo listened silently, he was not impressed; he couldn't fathom it. There was no evidence that Alex had anything to do with dead or stunned fish. He was endangering her life, for what? Matt argued that the Russians had to be up to something and they should try and find out what it was, perhaps there was a bigger picture to consider. Murdo disagreed.

"A bunch of coincidences don't make a hunch boy. Just do the job you have been asked to do. I seem to remember we had this problem with you last time, don't make me regret employing you. Get on with it! Get her out of there. This is simple; it is not for you to sort out their political games. I am not impressed with this, Matt." He hung up.

Matt considered. What was he to do? He actually understood why Murdo was angry, but didn't quite expect to be treated like a naughty school boy. Alex should have been safely in

Edinburgh now, sharing her secrets with the eager bureaucrats. He didn't like to think that he was endangering her life, Boris and Ivan didn't look the type to be messed around with.

He went back inside to look at the maps and charts. On the way in he met Alex in the corridor, followed inevitably, by the goons. As they passed she dropped some files on the floor. Being the gentleman, he sighed and bent down to help her pick them up. She muttered quickly "I give message to Donna. You talk to boy Carl." She moved away without a second glance, shoving her papers at Boris. Matt returned to his desk in the control room. He rifled through his files and found the exercise operating plan that showed maps and details of vessel movements. He sat in his chair not really paying attention at first, staring at the screens. He looked from screen to screen; oddly he couldn't see Carl in any of the operating areas. He must be here somewhere. He waited for a decent interval so as not to look suspicious and then went to look for him. Where would I go if I had just had a row with seniors and felt pissed off? He thought for a moment. He knew where to head for and this time his hunch was right.

Matt found the crew room in the back of the building. From the corridor it was just another nondescript doorway but once inside it was more homely. A large light rectangular room, the outside wall consisted mainly of old metal framed windows. The opposite wall held a long row of kitchen cupboards under a worktop that housed a sink and was decorated with an assortment of a microwave, kettles and a grill. At one end was a large screen TV which was quietly broadcasting the BBC news channel. At the other was a large metal cabinet, with one door hanging open, showing shelves piled high with chocolate bars, cans and crisps. They're prepared for a siege, thought Matt, or at least some long working hours. There was a couple of tables and an assortment of armchairs. The faded upholstery and worn carpet were testament to long usage.

One of the kettles had just boiled. Carl was randomly opening and shutting cupboard doors, looking but not looking. He had not noticed Matt enter the room; he was in his own world. They were alone in the room, no time to waste. Matt got two mugs out of the sink.

"Tea or coffee?" he asked, lifting a mug towards Carl. The young man didn't look round. He was short and stocky, built for stamina rather than speed. He had a mop of short but dishevelled curly hair. His coveralls were open to show tatty jeans and a Biffy Clyro tour T-shirt.

Carl finally noticed that he was not alone. "I'm looking for my Iron Bru, but some git has moved it. I should have stayed in bed, not my effing day." He looked round as he spoke and Matt could see the frustration etched in his usually cheerful face.

"What's going on?" Asked Matt. "I saw you arguing with the Russians, now the ROV launch is delayed... Is there a problem?"

Carl stood up and looked Matt up and down, weighing up what he should say. He knew of him locally, but didn't know him well. He understood that Matt was here to do some sort of report on the exercise. He didn't want to land the Range in bother, but didn't want the Range or more particularly himself being blamed for something he hadn't done.

"Look, maybe now's not the best time to talk to me, I'm a bit wound up and I don't need another lecture." He was saying the right thing, but just the very act of talking made the anger boil up again. He drew a long breath: "I'm not in the habit of causing international incidents and I'm not a liar or careless either. Somebody's at it and I'm the easy target to blame ... What really sucks is that the big man and that English git are not even prepared to listen to me. I'm the kid, just the apprentice, so obviously I must be wrong." He slammed the cupboard door and glared at Matt.

Matt spoke quietly and reassuringly. He explained that he was just trying to understand what the day to day issues were in an exercise, no big deal. People get stressed under the pressure and mistakes are made. To draw the boy out he stretched the truth slightly.

"I've just been speaking with Dr. Alex; it was her that said I should speak with you. She isn't blaming anything on you."

"Did she?" a glimmer of relief swept across the boy's face. "I was told that none of them trust me now. That is why I have been moved off control room duties. So that's good at least, she's smart. Unlike that arrogant so and so Wally, he'd be dangerous if he wasn't so stupid."

Matt hadn't spoken to anyone yet, the Range management had all been incommunicado, but he knew that he was about to get the inside track.

"I've been told not to talk to anyone..." began Carl.

"Absolutely, this is not something to be gossiped about, but look at this as part of the investigation. I will be reporting back, but I need to get all the facts."

"OK." He didn't need much encouragement. "It's quite simple really. I am... Was... Responsible for the pre and post operations check list. A cool way to be involved, but no big shakes. I recorded key readings to confirm readiness for operation. It's the Range's assurance that everything is as they say it is. I do the checks, give the results to Frank and he says they are good to go. Only today they weren't and somehow that's my fault."

Carl went on to explain the checks he undertook, that he noted the vital systems status to provide calibration and maintain the record of activity. "But the figures I took this morning didn't tie in with yesterday afternoon's. It was as if the ROV had been taken out for a spinny last night! Everyone went mad when I said this, said I was trying to cause an international incident to cover my mistakes. Everyone has had a go, telling me just to admit it, but I wouldn't. There is going to be an investigation, but meantime I'm off the team. Which means I can't get at the data of course to prove I'm right."

Matt felt sorry for Carl. The young man had been so pleased at being able to have such a central role; to have to bear such public humiliation was hard, especially if he was right. He thanked him for his cooperation and assured him that he would investigate it properly for him. His next step was to pin down Frank.

It took Matt a while to manage a conversation with Frank. He was busy re-arranging the day's activities to have minimum impact on the exercise. The use of the ROV had been pulled for that day due to "technical issues". By the time they sat down together in their shared office, Frank looked and sounded harassed, which wasn't like him. "I'm sorry, I haven't been avoiding you, it's just been hectic today on and off Range. International fall outs; staff issues and being blamed for off Range alleged incidents. It really has been one of those days; I'm expecting a plague of locusts next! It's annoying, especially after yesterday went so well."

As he spoke the light on his desk phone was flashing. "I've switched it to answer phone. I need at least ten minutes' peace."

That, thought Matt, is probably how long I've got then.

Despite his outburst, Frank didn't give much detail. He told Matt of stories about odd things happening with the wildlife near to a small island called Marolaig. "Questions are being asked, but then the fish magically got better...would you credit it? They don't understand how we work. I have explained that we are not operational overnight and on top of that there's a fish farm nearby that runs twenty-four / seven. I bet they aren't being quizzed, yet I still have to respond."

Matt had forgotten about the fish farm, they shouldn't be discounted, but was someone else busy last night?" he couldn't help but wonder.

Now in full swing, Frank continued his rant. "on top of that, the Russians have claimed that that they are being attacked by either the UK or American Secret Services. Here!". "The nearest thing we have to a spy is you and God knows that caused enough fuss."

"And as if that wasn't enough, the Americans have accused one of our apprentices of mucking up the daily calibration readings, so he is throwing his teddies about in the staff room."

Matt couldn't help but smile. He hoped he wasn't blushing. "You are not having a good day are you?"

If Carl was right he wasn't the only one active last night, but what were they up to, who was sabotaging who? Perhaps he needed to get onto the Range overnight.

Matt had itchy feet; he didn't want to stay in the control room waiting for something to happen. He needed more time with Carl and he needed to put a plan together, to sort this out and have a second attempt at getting Alex to the mainland. She would be being watched more closely now, so Stuart's boat still remained the best option, but he would have at least to have made some progress on the environmental problem before he could ask him to get ready again.

He decided to get out and about and use his Range pass to the full. He told Frank that he wanted to see how the trial was affecting the rest of the Range.

"I don't want to be in your hair, so can I have a wander round and see what everyone else is doing today? You know at the launch areas and in your shore-side compound?"

Frank was not comfortable with this. He appreciated the request but Matt would have to be escorted and Frank was tied to the control room as they were running late due to the morning's delay. Matt was not to be deterred, "This is the very time I would like to see. Couldn't someone else escort me? There must be someone spare?"

Franks phone seemed to be flashing even more vigorously, he glanced anxiously at it and took the bait. He could kill two birds with one stone, get a couple of hours off from babysitting Matt and get rid of Carl moping round the building with a face like a thunderstorm. Carl wouldn't be needed until after the day's trial was finished to shut down the control room, so he could lose him for a couple of hours.

"Hang on then, I will see what I can do; but for God's sake, keep out of trouble."

Half an hour later Matt was in the Range's land rover rolling out of the control building gates with Carl at the wheel. Matt had a plan, maybe he could get his evidence after all. He asked him to drive around onto the Machair and around the Range boundaries, so he could see the flags and observation points. It was a bit weak, but it got them out. At a quiet point he asked him to pull over.

Matt took a gamble. "Frank tells me you are a real electronics whiz. I think with your help, I've got a way of proving you right and finding out what is going on." Carl took the compliment without batting an eyelid. He nodded for Matt to continue.

"Is there any way we can take a feed from the ROV ops room and monitor it overnight. Like the one to the control room?"

"Are you mad?" Carl didn't answer initially; he just looked at Matt as if he had just offered him hard drugs.

"Do you have any idea what you are asking? I could lose my job or end up in prison."

He hasn't said no, thought Matt.

"Looks to me that your job isn't that secure right now. If you are right that someone was playing with the ROV last night, we need to know who and why. We also need to know if it had anything to do with the dead fish off Marolaig last night."

Carl was dismissive, "They're saying that didn't happen, just one of the Steele boys having a few too many bevies or if it did it was something to do with Marine Harvest."

"Aye, they're also saying you can't be trusted to read a couple of measurements. I think they're wrong about both things, but there's only one way to find out."

Carl didn't reply, he was looking down, fiddling with a loose thread on his jeans.

"If you told me the truth this morning, you'll be a hero and not sacked. I don't believe in coincidences. This is about more than you and my report. But then... if you can't do it..."

Carl pulled the thread sharply. "Let me think about it."

They drove on to the next observation point. Carl stayed in the car, while Matt went in and talked with the staff.

As Matt returned to the car he could see a change in Carl's body language. He was sitting up straighter and had a look of quiet determination about him.

"So what are we doing then?"

The young man gave him a half smile. "You're not letting this go are you?" He seemed more energised. "OK then, well, it is theoretically possible. We can take the feed that goes to the control room and redirect it anywhere we like but we can't get a feed off of site coz of the security wall. Also it will need to be accessed through a cleared laptop, like the ones in the control room that are password protected..."

"Like the one I've got in there?" Interrupted Matt.

"Yes, just like that one," agreed Carl cautiously.

~~~~~~~~~~~~~~~~~~~~~~~~~~~~~~~~~~~~~~

Chapter Ten: The Depot

The Range shore side compound was known as The Depot. It was a large engineering base that housed a number of support activities. The people that worked there did not have the same high tech facilities as their colleagues at the top of the hill and often felt like the poor relations. Matt and Carl drove the long way back to give them time to talk. They drove across the Machair using a network of ministry of defence metalled roads and local dirt tracks. The local crofters were paid an allowance by the government for use of the common grazing land. By the time they pulled up at the depot reception a plan was forming in Matt's mind.

Frank had phoned ahead so they were signalled to drive straight in by the guard as they both had Range passes.

Carl gave the guard a cheery wave. "That's a piece of luck, if they had wanted me to sign you in, it might have caused difficulties later." As agreed, Carl took Matt on a tour of the facility. Matt was surprised at the different activities that went on. Another legacy from the former RAF presence in Uist, the site was far larger than was visible from the road. It sprawled into the sand dunes housing hangars, workshops, and a dynamic support system that enabled Skip's proclamations in the windowless control room on the hillside above to become reality. Although the buildings looked like an unplanned collection of 1960s prefabs, they were linked by state of the art fibre optics. Carl joked that the company invested in the communications network rather than paint. Matt smiled, he suspected that like every squaddie considering the defence cuts, he knew how the staff felt about that!

Towards the back of the stores building there were some empty offices. Carl explained that a lot of people have in effect two jobs on Range. "They don't get paid twice though!" He opened a side door which led into a darkened hallway. "There are usually people working in here, but when trials are on they are seconded to act as part of the trials safety team." He opened an office door, to reveal a tidy desk in front of a small, high window. He made himself comfortable in a plush swivel chair. "This is Ronnie MacRury's office. It has several distinct advantages for us. Firstly it is out of the way and no one will see in that wee window; secondly I happen to know that Ronnie is at lookout station four, near Bornish and as his jacket isn't on that coat stand," Carl pointed to a rickety, mock -Victorian styled stand, with a variety of waterproofs on it, "he will be heading straight home from there at the end of the exercise, so it's all ours." Matt wondered how he could tell that a jacket was missing. But Carl continued.

"And thirdly;" he grinned as he theatrically opened the desk drawer and produced a well used cake tin. "His cake and biscuit collection is Range famous. I do hope he is more forgiving than Mike is." Matt was pleased to see that Carl was getting a bit of his spirit back. This might just work after all.

Matt made himself comfortable on the floor, out of sight, while Carl left and headed back up the hill to the Control Building. It was close to five o'clock. The exercise would be wrapping up soon and Carl would be needed to de-configure the control room.

On returning to the control room Carl told Frank that Matt had received a phone call after which he had asked to be dropped off at home. He was not coming back for the de-brief and would collect his car later. Carl had agreed to make sure Matt's work station was shut down as part of the general closing up. Frank thought this a bit odd and wondered what was so important. Matt seemed to be running all over the place and asking odd questions for someone who was meant to be just passively observing the trial. "Probably just bigging up his job," Frank thought unkindly.

Nobody noticed Carl as he went about his normal routine of closing down the control room work stations, nor when he casually slipped Matt's laptop into his rucksack. With the control room secured, he took his time and wandered round to the ROV operations room and logged onto the console. It didn't take him long to do what he needed to do. He had no way of checking if he had done it right. He also thought through how he would cover his footsteps so that people wouldn't notice the changes immediately in the morning. He knew that as soon as Matt logged on at an irregular access point it would be spottable, but he hoped it wouldn't be obvious straight away to give them time to sort out whatever was going on.

The minutes crawled by for Matt as he waited for Carl to return. He initially sat under the window, facing the clock. But it had been a long day, he had no idea what the next day would bring, so took the opportunity to rest his chin on his chest and get some sleep. As dusk fell, the camp closed down and as human activity ceased the building took on a life of its own. The old steel framework creaked as it cooled down and distant windows rattled like a convict dragging chains. A fax machine buzzed occasionally in another office, while the plumbing gurgled away to itself from time to time. Despite all this noise Matt knew the second that he was not alone.

The first sign he heard was scratching and rummaging behind the wall to the adjoining office followed by a skittering in the roof space. Something was running around above his head and there was definitely more than one. He shifted his position on the floor. The scuttling ceased. The rodents froze as they became aware of his presence. Then presently they scuttled away. Matt was sure he could hear them in the walls. He made a mental note to keep an eye out for mouse traps when he moved around the room. They need a cat he thought, probably several. He would make that recommendation in his report he thought as he dozed off.

Suddenly Matt was wide awake. Where was he? What time was it? He could hear voices. He froze as the rats had done earlier, hardly daring to breathe as he listened intently. There were voices in the corridor outside. Was this Ronnie coming back? Why would he return in the middle of the night? Could he roll under the desk? His mind raced. There were two people, they were discussing football, and trying the office doors. Matt realised it must be the guards on their regular night time patrol. How was he going to talk his way out of this? They were getting closer. As if in answer to his prayers there was the shrill sound of a mobile phone. (Huh, thought Matt, they are allowed them!)

"Depot Security", a voice said loudly in the corridor. "Hang on, I'll step outside to take this, the signal is grotty in these old buildings." The guard moved away, Matt could hear the mutterings of the conversation. It wasn't long before his colleague joined him. Perhaps he didn't like being alone with the beasties in the building.

A little later Carl was at the site's main gate, talking his way back onto site. It wasn't so uncommon for the electronics and instrumentation staff to turn up to do overnight maintenance or checks on the communications or IT equipment especially during exercises. The problem was that the guards were usually notified in advance. Carl felt like a criminal, this went against the grain. Here goes bluffing it he thought. He rationalised that if he was caught now the contents of his rucksack were more likely to get him fired than fibbing to a guard.

As pre-planned with Matt, Carl walked in to the warm guard room as if he was expected.

"Hi guys, sorry to wake you!" He was pleased to see that it was two of the guards whom he knew quite well. This wouldn't be easy, they took their jobs seriously, but they all had been briefed on the importance of the exercise, so maybe he could get them to see the bigger picture. He was aware that he would only have one shot at it and he would be found out by morning. But by then, if Matt was right, he would have evidence of his own. He was nervous, but he had to go for it.

The guards had seen his car pull in and were waiting for him.

"Is this a social call Carl? We weren't expecting visitors."

"Very funny. I've had a bad enough day already, please don't wind me up."

One guard flicked through his day sheet, while the other sat at his PC to check visitor requests.

"Nope, son, sorry. Nobody has told us anything."

Matt shook his head and sucked his teeth loudly. "Bloody effing typical. I knew he had it in for me!" the guards looked confused.

"Sorry, sorry, I shouldn't swear at you. It's just so frustrating and I'm going to get the blame again." He emphasised the last word.

"They decided this afternoon that they needed someone to do sustainability checks on several random access points overnight because of communications problems reported by the French today. It's a shit job cos you're up half the night and have to sit for ages watching laptops spew out codes."

The guards nodded sympathetically, even though they didn't really know what Carl was on about.

"Anyway, the only reason it's me is because I am being blamed for the cock up this morning. Scapegoat, then punished for something I didn't do. Now, cos they were too busy lecturing me instead of doing the paper work the tests can't be done, so that's me in the shit again. Situation normal, eh?"

Carl looked fed up. The story of some sort of issues with the ROV had filtered round the camp, the guards felt sorry for him.

"Look, you know that the visitor notifications are routed centrally, through the security system. With the amount of traffic at the moment, they are very low priority, if he did it late, it might not come through till tomorrow."

"Aye, it probably was after five by the time he stopped moaning".

The two guards looked at each other.

"You've got your swipe card to get you into the buildings you need?"

Carl nodded.

The two guards looked at each other.

"He can't get into anywhere he shouldn't."

"No, and the notification will probably be here by the morning." They were talking themselves into doing the lad a favour.

Everyone had been briefed on the importance of the exercise and that it needed to run smoothly. No-one wanted to foul things up. It didn't even cross their minds that the young man in front of them might have re-programmed his security access.

Just to be on the safe side Carl didn't drive directly to where Matt was waiting. Just in case they decided to watch or follow, he didn't want to ruin it now.

It was with relief that Matt heard Carl pull up outside. He was past worrying. There was only a short list of people who would be dropping by. The building noises ceased as Carl noisily entered the building. His arms full with his laptop and assorted cabling he allowed the doors to slam behind him. He came in backwards pushing the door open with his back. He leant towards the wall and pressed the light switch with his forehead, obviously used to carting such equipment about. Matt squinted at the sudden brightness.

"I haven't woken you have I?"

"No such luck. Did you have any trouble getting in?"

"Not really, but we will have to be nippy speaking with Frank in the morning, because they will follow up with him."

"Aye, OK." Matt hoped he could keep his word. "Let's get this party started then."

They set up the laptop and docking station on the desk as if Carl were carrying out his normal routine tests. The apprentice was sitting at the desk, while Matt stayed on the floor, not immediately obvious if somebody did come in. To minimise any reflected light Matt had pulled the blind on the little window earlier; they didn't want to be interrupted now. They were initially full of optimism that they would be able to log in quite quickly, but of course it wasn't that simple.

After what seemed like hours of agonising faffing about Carl managed to connect to the feed from the ROV room but something was obviously wrong. He re-checked everything yet again, "Shit, shit, shit," he muttered. He tried various configurations but couldn't improve upon it. He looked as if he was about to weep, he was devastated. The problem was that they didn't have the view of the room that they were hoping for, the one that Matt had seen from the control room. They were connected to something, but Carl wasn't exactly sure what.

"I'm really sorry mate. I was so nervous that someone would ask what I was doing, I must have missed something, or someone has switched it all off, I dunno." His youth showed through, his shoulders were slumped like a despairing child.

"But you have something don't you?" Matt felt desperate too, but needed to keep Carl focussed if they were going to achieve anything. The young man scratched his head then fiddled again with the keyboard. "I think this is the maintenance connection to the ROV. I switched it on, cos it runs in the background, while other operations are going on. Unless the pilot notices it, we will see the camera feed, operating instructions and communications as text boxes. No sound though. I plugged it in as a backup. Just as well I did." He sat back in his chair and sighed. "Problem is; we won't know until someone switches the thing on."

"That's perfect, it's all we need. If we can prove its being operated overnight and where it goes, we can see if there is a link or not to the dead fish." Matt tried to reassure him.

"Aye and prove that I didn't screw up yesterday, save my job and show that Hank is a lying bastard." It wasn't that Carl didn't believe Matt's story about the link to the dead fish, but he was far more interested in proving his innocence. Even so, he was not optimistic. "As long as it is switched on, that is."

"All we can do is wait." Matt gave the young man an encouraging smile as he shuffled himself into a more comfortable position on the floor. "Try and take five now, hopefully we will have work to do later."

And so they waited.

They didn't sleep, but talked quietly about life, the universe and everything. Matt retold what he and Stuart had witnessed. He mentioned that it was near to Marolaig, but didn't explain why he had been there at that time in the morning, which would have seemed odd in the middle of an important exercise.

He was not sure why, but Carl got the impression that there was more to Matt's interest than his Range report. It explained why, unlike many others, Matt believed what Stuart Steele had reported. It puzzled Carl as to why and who else was there, but he didn't ask. Matt explained that he expected to see the Russians trying to sabotage another country's vessel or equipment. This didn't explain the Americans odd reaction, but maybe he was trying to cover a mistake of his own that had let the Russians in. They had the ship AIS and Range charts open and spread out on the desk so as to be able to identify and warn of potential targets.

All at once the screen came to life.

Matt pulled up a chair next to Carl as they watched as somebody was working their way through the start up checks. They obviously knew what they were doing. Matt and Carl didn't speak, waiting to see if the maintenance connection would be noticed. Whoever was operating appeared far more proficient with its operation than they had been during the day.

"They're not that good, they don't know we're here," whispered Carl with a quiet smile. Pointing at the laptop, he talked Matt through the numbers that were being displayed on a side panel of the dark screen. They showed the engine revolutions, speed, depth and direction. Numbers and coordinates were being programmed in. There was an empty box in the bottom right hand corner.

"That's the voice recognition system. If they use the comms system, it will show up as text in there".

"It's very dark."

"The camera will come on when they start moving, though the water will be dark so I don't know how much we will actually see." Both men were still whispering.

Another window opened up on the screen. The operator was calling up maps from another data base. Carl and Matt rummaged through the paper work on the desk, they didn't recognise it. It was not within the Range boundary.

"Look at it. Can we enlarge it? That's not a military map, well not one used since Hadrian was a boy." It was nothing like Matt had seen before.

"It does look kinda old," agreed Carl. He started searching on his phone to try and find something similar. "We'll get the coordinates when they plug them in, but it is bizarre. What are they up to?"

"It doesn't look like anywhere on Range. Shit, we may have been right about the fish."

In the bottom corner of the screen the communications came to life. Words started to appear. They were calling someone.

~~~~~~~~~~~~~~~~~~~

Chapter Eleven: Here there be monsters

The text came up in HTML script, with little differentiation between question and answer. Matt and Carl had to concentrate to follow it.

Confirm status?

Checks completed, we are ready to proceed

Good. You have the new coordinates.

Yes. A little difficulty getting the map, but we are all set.

Matt nudged Carl. "Quick, get a screen shot of that map before it disappears." Carl did so as they continued following the conversation.

If it proves positive, do you have the recovery plan in place?

Yes. Will send photographs tonight. If positive we will create a diversion on the MoD Range tomorrow, followed by recover during the day.

What is the diversion?
Accuse the scientist of sabotage, the boy of incompetence and the Range of environmental negligence. Spark an international dispute to halt the exercise, so no interference. They will be so wrapped up in themselves that they will not notice or care about us.

Good hunting.

The text box dimmed. Matt and Carl just looked at each other. Neither had been sure what they would find, but it had not been this. They searched the origin of the map as its image disappeared from the screen. Co-ordinates were typed in and the ROV slowly began to move.

Matt typed the co-ordinates into the maps stored on his phone. He showed them to Carl. They both recognised where the vessel was going, they just didn't understand why.

Fascinated, the boys watched as the ROV silently made its way out to sea. The camera gave a murky view of the ocean. It was dark and forbidding, showing only the occasional fish scurrying past or the slap of a branch of slimy seaweed as it was knocked aside.

"Is that it?" Squinted Matt. "Surely the image gets better than this?"

"Yep, this is just in transit mode. It illuminates and focuses when it locks onto a target or target area for a search."

"Hmm," muttered Matt. "Is illuminating the posh name for killing fish? We need to find out what the target is."

They started by researching the co-ordinates, then points along the sheltered, rocky east coast of South Uist, but found nothing that made sense to be sending an unmanned submarine to examine. Carl then downloaded the screenshot of the map. At last they had a result, but it still wasn't one that made sense.

"OK, I can confirm it's old." Carl was peering at the screen. "I think I am suffering from sleep deprivation.... It says here it was drawn in 1620. I must have got something wrong."

"No, hold the bus... There's a description... ahh... it's in Gaelic.... it's been a while since I tried to read any, apart from the hymns in church, Can you?"

Matt lent over, squinted and mouthed the words aloud. "I'm not that good either, but I really don't recognise some of those words, must be very old, or Irish or something...can you search on the title?"

Carl searched again and laughed. "You won't believe this. We've now got a poem in the old language .... Shall I ring someone from the college or Ceolas maybe?"

Carl pressed Print on his phone which started a whirring and clicking in an adjoining room as the department printer came to life. Matt was racking his brains, where did he unexpectedly see someone from Ceolas recently? Out of place, but somehow related. He felt it was important, but he couldn't think. He was getting tired too. He stared at the verse, the odd word looked familiar, but he could not make sense of it.

Fon fhairge fheargach gu Siar

Tha ionmhas mòr na Rìoghachd

Air a dhìon leis na fir bheag ghorm

Bho shùilean meallta, eudmhor

Thoir an aire, ma ghoideas tu m' òr,

Cha dèan e feum no fortan dhut

Thèid do bhàthadh, cruaidh 's fuar

Is bidh do chridhe san teine mhòr.

"Well, it's something about the sea and hell." Muttered Carl,

"And the wee blue men, but I thought they were from Lewis." Matt pretended surprise when it was clear that Carl did not know what he was talking about. He was about to explain when something caught his attention. He glanced quickly at the ROV screen but it was still dark. His senses heightened. There it was again, covered by the noise of the printer. Was it footsteps outside? Carl had heard it too. Matt sprinted to the only halfway decent hiding place possible in the office. Carl pulled himself up to the desk. He quickly shoved both their phones into his pockets and shuffled the maps and papers together. He pulled the laptop towards him and tried to feign an expression of tired boredom.

Matt was standing behind the door, having pulled the laden coat stand in front of himself. It didn't exactly hide him, but made him less obvious, or at least so he hoped. They stared at each other silently as they listened to the building door creak open and footsteps pad down the hallway towards them.

"What you doing down here laddie? We've been searching all over for you." Eddie the younger of the two guards stood in the doorway. He was a part time Special Constable, so Carl knew he wouldn't miss much, but hopefully he wasn't looking for anything.

"Well, I had to use a docking station that was likely to have poor comms and, well, as you know this old part of camp is terrible. But more importantly, I knew where the best biscuit stash is, so it was a no brainer."

The guard remained in the doorway, inches away from Matt, who was holding his breath, trying to stay perfectly still.

"Is that you using the printer too? I heard it as I came in."

"Yeah, come and have a look at this." Carl seized the opportunity to lead Eddie out of the room. Matt still dare not move.

"It's been such a bitch tonight. I have to put all the protocols in place and then let it run for an hour to confirm everything is OK. It gets to about forty five minutes then crashes. I tweak a few nodes and then try again, but it doesn't want to play. I am getting really fed up."

Eddie was more interested in the printer, he picked the sheet of paper out of the machine and was looking at it. Carl hoped that he wasn't really listening to the rubbish he was spouting.

"As you can see I was getting bored and doing some surfing to keep me awake. Came across this, it's meant to be about the waters off the east side, I've printed it off for granny, thought she'd like it. Can you read it? I couldn't understand all of it. Looks like something out of Lord of the Rings!"

Obviously relieved that he hadn't caught Carl printing off some official secrets, Eddie relaxed slightly. "No but Seamus might know, he's in the car. I'll just call him in."

"I didn't hear a car, where are you parked?"

"No he's just outside. We have the electric ones now. They're better for the environment and the bad guys or skiving apprentices won't hear us coming. Well that's the theory anyway." He laughed, but Carl wasn't taking the bait.

"Cool! Can I have a look? A bit of fresh air will do me good."

They went outside where Seamus and Eddie showed off their new Nissan Leaf telling Carl how far it went and how easy it was to charge. Seamus looked at the poem. "Blimey that's a bit grim! He tried to read it out loud in English to Carl, but didn't get very far.

"Something about the seas off the islands.

Yep, and maybe hidden treasure?

I recognise the wee blue men,

Something about eyes.

 A threat about taking some gold and it will not be a good thing.

Then it says about your body being dead and cold,

The last Line is...Your heart will go to hell."

"Can I keep this?" He asked, "I'll see if I can find anything about it. I'll show it to Sarah MacDonald from the College. She's bound to be able to translate it and might know a bit about the history."

"*Mòran taing,*" agreed Carl. "That would be fine, I'll print another one. I'd be interested in what she thinks. Listen I had better stop skiving and get back to work if I am going to get any shut eye before the morning. I will give you a shout on my way out." Carl gave them a cheery wave as he headed back to the office. He was surprised to see Matt sitting at the desk staring intently at the now lit screen.

"Quick," hissed Matt, "look at this!"
The sea bed had been illuminated giving a window into another world. Against the backdrop of the dark ocean it had an alien, almost space like quality. There was a night vision filter on the camera lens that rendered the meandering fish and floating kelp a neon green.

125

The seaweed looked as if it was dancing, swaying to unheard music. As the camera panned around, the background shapes appeared too dark; this gave them a menacing quality as is they were coming towards you. Other objects seemed to glisten. It must from the lights on the craft thought Matt; it surely couldn't be moon light. He wondered how deep they were. He pointed to the co-ordinates to confirm where they were. Both men were mesmerised as the scene in front of them unfolded. Matt, who had dived before, had never seen the seabed like this. Suddenly the camera halted. It zoomed in. Slowly, out of the murky gloom appeared a distinctive shape. Despite the seaweed, there was a line the eye could follow. It didn't look natural; could it be manmade? What had they found?

The controller obligingly manoeuvred the ROV around their discovery. Matt tried to process what he could see. Whatever the structure was, it had been there a long time. It was tangled up in plants and was obviously home to a variety of sea creatures and coral. Both men peered hard at the screen, not believing what they were seeing. It looked like a wooden structure, possibly forty foot long. Even through the water they could see amazing detail.

The ROV manoeuvred around the object and down to one side. "I think it's a Birlinn, a mediaeval sailing boat," whispered Matt, in awe, "look, she's lying on her side." He traced the outline of the frame on the screen. What must have been the gunwale was intact. You could see gaps that could have been for oars that now had long trails of weed spilling out of them. The still graceful curve ended in a carved knotted figure head, in the shape of a Celtic cross. As the camera swept the underside they were able to make out other markings. Along the upper hull there were carvings of tiny figures, masts, sails and weapons all still preserved in their watery grave. Matt would have been happy to examine them further, but the ROV controller had other things in mind. He turned above the wreck, tilting the camera downward so that they could see into the vessel. It was generally open, with what looked like slats or the remains of wooden thwarts across the frame. Debris underneath them had piled up over the years.

"Where does all that rubbish come from?" asked Carl. He rubbed his eyes, not sure if he believed what he was seeing.

The ROV operator was panning slowly. He zoomed in, but as he did so the scene changed from fascinating to macabre.

"Oh god, what's that? Look what's happening," gasped Carl. Despite the magnificent sight, both men wanted them to stop.

"They needed to turn the radar off or down or something" Carl was pointing at the screen in despair . The sad spectacle of suspended, stunned fish began to fill the screen, dropping onto the ancient ship. Even from a distance it made the boys choke. The murder of the innocents.

Whoever was in control of the camera had no such scruples. There was something glinting under the benches. It was an odd shape, but it was a regular shape. It was about six inches long, cylindrical. The boys were puzzled. It didn't look like a weapon; could it be jewellery? It looked as if it was attached to something.

It was hard to see."Looks like a hinge?" Carl wanted the camera man to change angle so that he could get a better view.

"Possibly, could be bronze maybe," agreed Matt. "Is that the outline of some sort of chest in the shadow?"

Whoever was operating the ROV must have come to the same conclusion and having identified his prize, made a quick decision. They were not hanging about, the camera was shut down quickly and the radar switched off. The ROV turned, the boys watched the coordinates for the Range being entered, it was heading for home. The text box in the corner of the screen lit up and the words "mission accomplished" appeared. The vehicle was moving quickly now.

They disconnected the maintenance feed. For a few seconds they sat, stunned, trying to comprehend what they had just seen. Carl began to pack the laptop up. Both of them were aware that they now had work to do.

"I need to get all this sorted and back before the morning brief and set up tomorrow or they'll never believe that I'm not a spy. What are you going to do?"

"I need to work out who it was that was driving that sub and who they were talking to, but that should become clear in the morning and then I'm going to catch them." His brain was working overtime. Was the other person on the island, on one of the boats in the exercise or somewhere else completely? The potential scale of what they were facing worried him. He took a deep breath, the first thing was to sort what was on his door step. He must understand the origin of the map if he was to have any chance of persuading Alex to wait another day and that would be a start; but neither of them had much time.

"Let's get out of here," suggested Matt. "I really need to think."

Matt climbed into the boot of Carl's car and they drove back round towards the gate.

It was almost dawn as Carl slowed down to wave a weary good night to the guard. Seamus signalled for him to stop. Carl wondered if they had been rumbled as the guard walked purposefully towards the car with a piece of paper on his hand.

"I messaged Sarah, I'm sure she'll get back to you when she sees it. I found your poem and a bit about it though." He waved the piece of paper triumphantly.

"It was in the Carmina Gadelica ... There was some Irish lord in Donegal in the 1600s who sent his daughter with her dowry, to the islands to be married to some chief. Anyway, the boat was supposed to have been lost somewhere between the Sound of Barra and Uist. The father was told it was in a storm, but he always suspected that the boat was sunk, his treasure stolen and his daughter murdered. He pronounced a curse on anyone who robbed her grave. There's even a map somewhere showing where people think the wreck is!"

"Is there?" beamed Carl. His gratitude was more heartfelt and genuine than Seamus could know.

Matt could hear the conversation in the boot. One of the puzzle pieces from earlier in the week fell into place. The Carmina Gadelica; that was the book he had seen in the control room. He knew that he had recognised it; it was in the school library. But who else had been doing their homework?

Chapter Twelve: The morning after the night before.

Matt got home in the early hours of the morning. He felt rough and grubby; he suspected that he looked as much. He was stiff from having travelled home in the boot of Carl's car. He was running on adrenalin from the lack of two night's sleep, which was making him feel agitated. He needed to wind down and think clearly.

There were several messages on his phone. Matt's sense of foreboding increased when he realised that two of the missed calls were from Marieke and Kate. He could have kicked himself. He was pleased that Marieke at least had left a message that meant that she was OK, didn't it? He tried to check what time she had left the message at, but he knew that this wasn't reliable in the islands. He replayed the message several times. She just said hello and asked him to give her a call. She wasn't one for small talk and her tone seemed neutral. There was nothing there to be worried about, but she didn't mention where she was or Kate's invite... Not even to nag him about interfering. He felt unsettled. He almost rang them back, but finally decided that they both would probably be asleep at this time in the morning and would not thank him.

The second actual message was an incoherent colourful rant from Stuart. Matt was not surprised to hear that he had found more areas of dead and stunned fish. When he returned the call he was relieved just to get his friend's answer service as he didn't want to get involved in long explanations, not yet anyway. He confirmed that he now knew what was happening. He arranged to meet with him mid morning.

"Have the boat fuelled *Ma tha* and be prepared for all possibilities. We're going fishing!"

The third call was unexpected, it was from Donna and she sounded uncharacteristically scared, as agitated as he felt himself. The message was odd in that it asked him to ring back, no matter what the time. So he called.

She must have been waiting for his call because she answered after half a ring. Donna told him that everyone had been arguing about the potential environmental fish issues. It got heated when Ivan and Boris turned on Alex. They had accused her of liaising with the yanks and being a spy who was trying to bring Mother Russia into disrepute somehow by causing an environmental issue that Russia would be blamed for.

"She was all over the place Matt," Donna explained. "She is terrified. She knows nothing about dead fish, she says she has to leave because of dead children and they are using this fish problem as a cover up to get rid of her."

"Dead Children? What dead children?"

"She said she didn't have time to tell you. It's what is going on at the university."

"What?"

"Well in short; apparently they are telling local peasant kids that they will take them on scholarships to give them a start in life. Then they say they are taking them away for some sort of work placements, but instead they are stealing their organs for the black market. You know, their kidneys and their eyes. They have been dumping the bodies in the Siberian desert."

"Bloody hell!"

"She reported them, but was told to leave it be. She went to the police and politicians but they didn't care. She made leaflets to warn the villagers. That's when things started getting nasty for her."

"So what's happening now?"

"Well, Boris and Ivan said that they had been given instructions. They were going to publicly condemn the yanks today. Then fly out immediately and withdraw their warship from the exercise as they did not want to be part of this. Alex has to go with them. If she attempts to speak with anyone or resist in any way, she will be stowed on their boat and made to return one way or another! She wants out now! I know she's some big shot clever scientist, but the lassie's greetin'. You have to do something Matt; she's scared for her life."

Matt felt really bad. He hadn't realised that it was so desperate for Alex and now things were getting even more complicated. No wonder she hadn't wanted to turn around in the Minch and come back. The Russians suspecting the Americans, that was an interesting concept... or were they playing a double bluff to divert suspicion, or were afraid that they were about to get caught. The only thing to do was to stick to the plan and go there and see who turns up. But it looked like he would have to take Alex with him. Oh well, at least he could tell Murdo that he was keeping her safe. He didn't know how Stuart would feel.

Matt had been lost in his own thoughts and hadn't realised that Donna was still talking.

"I know it's daft, but the Yanks have been acting very oddly. Wally got really pissed and was bragging about finally being able to be a somebody in his own right and that he would "Show her." I'm not saying that he has been doing stuff to the fish, but he is up to something."

Donna confirmed that she would see Alex at breakfast. Matt asked her to pass the message to Alex to play along with Ivan and Boris, to try and find out how much they knew if she could. She was to come to the morning brief and that he would get her out. She was to tell her to try and get to the bathroom or at least into the corridor of the control building by herself when he gave the signal and he would arrange the rest. Donna assured him that she would pass the message on as best she could.

"Don't leave it too long, Matt. She is really frightened."

Matt hung up. He now had to work out what was going on and how he was going to get Alex away. He was going to need Carl's help again too. He made a cup of coffee, opened his laptop and sat down at the kitchen table. He intended to start researching shipwrecks; instead he fell asleep in the chair.

Matt could smell bacon, or was it sausages? Was he dreaming? Whatever it was it smelled amazing. It took him a moment to get his bearings. He slowly opened his eyes. With all the angst that had been rushing through his brain the sight of his mum cooking at the stove and listening to the strains of BBC Radio Nan Gael were somehow comforting and normal. She noticed that he was awake.

"*Madainn mhath, Ciamar a tha thu?*"

"I'm Ok mum. Just missing a bit of sleep that's all."

"I guessed that. This job doesn't appear to be as straight forward as you first thought eh? Either that or you've been burning the candle at both ends with young Stuart?"

"Chance would be a fine thing."

"Go on and have a shower. Your breakfast will be ready when you come down. It will give you a second wind and set you up for the day."

Matt wearily pulled himself to his feet. He walked over and wrapped his arms round her shoulders. "Thanks mum," he murmured.

She hugged him back. "See, even James Bond needs his mother. A good breakfast inside you and you'll sort them all out!"

"Aye mam, I sure will." Matt felt better already as he climbed the stairs. He knew now what he had to do.

Feeling refreshed, Matt got to the Range early. He had talked his mum into giving him a lift and went to wait in his car until he saw Carl arrive. He was grateful for the fact that Seonag didn't ask him too many questions. She just pecked him on the cheek and left him there, saying that she would pray for him. "I may need that," he thought.

Just as he settled down, his phone rang. He didn't recognise the number. Who could be calling him at this time of the morning?

"*Feasgair Math, MacCaulay, Ciamar a tha sibh?*"

"Hi ya Sarah, didn't expect to hear from you quite so early, but thank you."

"Well, you got me intrigued. I woke up this morning to my phone beeping. I had been sent a poem, with a message attached to call Carl MacPhee. I've just spoken with him and he wanted me to speak with you urgently. What is going on? When did you guys get interested in history and why on earth is a 15th century poem so urgent?"

"Aw Sarah, it's a very long story, which I don't think you'd believe if I told you right now. But did you manage to translate it? Do you know anything about it?"

"I'm a linguist Matt, not a historian. You should talk with Ceolas or the like. But yes, I can read it... we will have to have a talk about why you can't, though." She laughed.

"There are lots of tales of shipwrecks round our shores," she continued. "You'll remember the trade route from Donegal to Lochboisdale was thriving. They were all related after all. The South end was the gateway to all the Outer Isles. They did it in the old fashioned open boats, Birlinns. Quite amazing really. Calmac can't get across the Minch to Lochboisdale if it's cloudy! All sorts of trade, conspiracies and politics went on. Looks like your poem refers to one potential deal that got sunk so to speak. There is a story about a young princess who was travelling from Ireland to be the bride of a Laird or someone up in Lewis. She would have been travelling up the east coast but she never got there for whatever reason. Her father is said to have cursed anyone who disturbs her grave, or probably more truthfully, stole his gold. So if you have found something you will have to be careful. You have to take these things with a pinch of salt though, there are also meant to be wee blue men and kelpies out there. I do hope not. Tell you what, give me your email and I'll translate the poem this morning for you then send it through. That OK?"

"Aye, that will be perfect thank you."

"On condition mind, that I get a cut if you have found something," she joked.

"Well, it will only be after SNH get their hands on it, mind. I'd appreciate it if you could keep this quiet as it's a bit sensitive at the moment."

"Stop the bus, you have found something! Don't worry, my lips are sealed. Nobody would believe me anyway."

She hung up. Matt was happy that he could trust Sarah. He remembered her as a couple of years ahead of him at school. She worked promoting Gaelic culture and language and was involved in a number of community projects. He wondered how much she would piece together, but was sure that she would keep it to herself, at least for now.

Carl arrived not long afterwards; he was fresh faced, but somewhat worried looking. Talking quietly in the car park, Matt explained that he was going to play on the fact that Ivan and Boris did not suspect him. They did not know that they had been watched. He needed a distraction to be able to get Alex away from them and asked Carl to be that distraction.

The young man creased his brow. He looked worried at first, but was still willing to help. Matt didn't want to go into details about things he didn't really understand but just made it clear that Alex was not part of whatever was going on, but her life was in danger if Matt left her there with them.

"Looks like I have no choice then," Carl agreed, but there was obviously something else bothering him as well. He was shuffling his feet in the dirt intently studying something on the ground. "It's just that I am worried about how all this is gonna pan out. Never mind what we saw, Mike isn't gonna be happy about what we did last night. It's me that works here... well for now anyway."

"It's about just keeping our nerve." Matt reassured him, he did understand the boy's concerns. "I'll square things with Frank just now and I have a couple of government friends who will thank you and make sure Mike knows to thank you too. C'mon, you don't want to let them get away with it do you?"

"No." He bucked up a bit. "I bloody don't. So what is it you want me to do again?"

Matt smiled. "That's down to you really, but I had this idea of you losing it at being accused of mucking things up. I need a diversion. How much of a drama queen can you be?"

"Huh, won't take much for me to tell who's doing this exactly what I think of them. I don't even know if I'm going to be allowed into the brief though."

"I'll see to that."

Carl gave Matt a tight smile as he walked away.

"This should be fun," muttered Matt as he grabbed his bag and followed the young man into the building.

Frank had arrived early too. Matt had noticed his car in the car park. He was on the phone when Matt entered the office. He had his head in his hand as he was talking. Despite his smart suit he had a ragged look about him, obviously unhappy about something. He hasn't had much sleep either, thought Matt. There was a desk in the office for Matt. He put his rucksack on it and turned and shut the door. He pulled over a chair and sat opposite Frank. He folded his arms and waited for him to finish talking.

Frank threw Matt a couple of exasperated looks. "I'll catch you later," he mouthed at one point trying to wave him away. Matt pursed his lips and shook his head.

"No, sorry. We need to talk now *Ma tha*."

It took Frank a couple of minutes to finish the call. The normally laid back engineer was looking stony faced and increasingly stressed. He was not having a good day.

"Everyone is up in arms. There has been another area of dead and stunned sea life found off the east coast. The rumour mill is in overdrive with all sorts of accusations being made. Skip wants to stop the exercise to show we are taking it seriously. Mike says that would be an admission of guilt and we should continue as it obviously has nothing to do with us. Skip isn't happy. So Matt, unless what you're about to ask is of earth shattering importance, I really don't have time. There's a lot going on. There have been too many odd things happening, people are asking difficult questions that we don't have answers for. I'm firefighting here. It's a terrible thing that's happening. Maybe Skip has a point."

"I'm not here to ask about it. I'm here to tell you at least a bit about what is going on. Not earth shattering, but may help you with your fires and save lives, both human and animal."

Frank was looking at the younger man differently now. His eyes narrowed as he pulled his chair closer to the desk.

"Go on then."

Matt had decided to keep things simple. He had tried to ring Murdo from his car earlier, but typically he was not able to get hold of him when he wanted him. So he was on his own. He had decided that a tale of hidden treasure would not be taken seriously by Frank or anyone else. So he decided to keep it simple, share the information that would keep the range on side and get Frank to cooperate with him.

"OK, I am going to be brief, as you're right, we really don't have a lot of time. There are some bits you are just going to have to trust me on, at least for now." He held Frank's gaze, willing him to accept and agree with what he was about to say.

"Thing is, just witnessing this exercise was only part of my brief for being here. I'm sorry, I am not at liberty to tell you my full brief."

Franks eyes had widened, he leaned forward waiting for Matt to continue.

"Two things have transpired that we need to deal with. The first is that one of the participants is attempting to undermine the exercise and UK MoD by causing these environmental incidents. They are going to blame the Range, probably at the morning brief in about half an hour and attempt to cause an international incident." Frank looked as if he was about to interrupt, but Matt continued.

137

"I also have very strong reason to believe that Dr. Alex's life is in serious danger. She is not part of the plot, but has incriminating evidence. She has already been threatened."

Frank's eyes were now even wider; his jaw had dropped involuntarily. "Can't we just arrest them, now, before the meeting? Keep this thing low key. I need to call Mike and Skip." He reached for the phone.

"No," replied Matt. He placed his hand on Frank's arm. "It's not that straightforward." Frank pulled his arm away, but did not go for the phone again. Matt nodded in unspoken thanks and continued.

"The problem is, although we know what is happening, because we have monitored communications, we don't actually know who is behind it. If they think we are onto them they will disappear off into the ocean. I need them to think that they are getting away with it."

Frank looked confused and made to interrupt.

"I will explain later, you can tell Mike and Skip what you like once I've left, we haven't got time now. I need to get Dr. Alex out of here. I need to be sure that whoever is behind this doesn't know that they've been rumbled. Once they think they've got away with it, I'm going to where that patch of dead fish is and I'm going to catch them at it."

Matt could almost see Frank digesting the information, his face spoke volumes. The confusion changed to anger and upset, but thankfully his face set in an expression of resolve and determination.

"So if you don't want me to alert management, what do you want me to do?"

"We do need to keep it as real as possible; I need Skip to be outraged. The Range is going to be told that it is down to Carl Mac Phee's incompetence and that he is involved. He isn't, I've warned him and asked him to react. Can you ensure he is there?"

Matt went onto explain what he wanted Frank to do. He also assured that him that he would take responsibility for any communications irregularities within the Range over the last twenty four hours. He felt he could buy time by not directly implicating Carl until all could be explained. Frank looked even more perplexed. But while still unhappy, Matt could see that he was making up his mind to help.

"You are really sure about this?"

"As sure as I can be. It's no good just stopping them, I want to catch them. I don't want the Range blamed, but I really don't want anyone hurt or our waters contaminated. Don't you agree?"

"Yes, but..."

Frank was interrupted by the Tannoy. "Morning brief starts at 0900 hours. All participants to make their way to the main conference room immediately." They had run out of time.

"Let's go. You know what to do."

"Yes, good luck and stay safe."

"Don't worry, I will. This is the bit I am good at."

~~~~~~~~~~~~~~~~~~~~

Chapter Thirteen: Another morning brief.

Matt and Frank walked round the building, shortly to join a subdued queue making their way into the conference room. They were talking in hushed voices, grim faced and jumpy, looking round, listening for snippets of information.

"This is terrible," remarked Frank. "To all intents and purposes the exercise is going so well, but the stories about another environmental incident are making everyone tense, it's amazing how word spreads so fast, even when they claim not to be able to understand each other half the time."

As they shuffled forward Matt scanned the group for sight of Alex. He had let her know through Donna what he needed her to do; he just hoped that she had got the message straight.

As everyone finally took their seats Frank earned a hard look from Skip as he insisted on taking a particular seat, one away from Carl, opposite Matt. This left two seats and then a separate single seat left for the three Russians. Things were bad enough; Skip couldn't understand why Frank would want to antagonise them any further. Mike wasn't pleased that Carl had been allowed to attend the meeting after his spat with the Americans the previous day. The atmosphere was wired with tension as Skip finally stood up to call the meeting to order.

In his usual direct manner, Skip told the meeting that the Director would start with a statement regarding the "Environmental issues" and the UK MoD's view on it. He said that they wanted to dispel any rumours and clear the air so that they could find an agreed way forward and get back to the matters in hand. Matt couldn't help but think that every word was going to be carefully scripted.

Mike stood, nodded to Skip and cleared his throat. He held a single typed sheet of paper in his hand.

"Firstly, I want to say on behalf of myself and every member of my staff, how shocked and appalled we are at the environmental incidents that have occurred over the last couple of days. Fishing and care for the island waters are an intrinsic part of our way of life and it is deeply upsetting to all of us. That said, the incidents have taken place in areas outside of our boundaries and, as far as we can tell, at times when the Range has been non operational. We are working closely with the Joint Warrior Management Committee, The Maritime and Coastguard Agency, the Department of Fisheries and Scottish Natural Heritage, offering them any assistance we can give to get to the bottom of it. There are, I must stress, no links between this exercise and the deaths of any fish and sea mammals." He paused and looked around the room. "This is however an extremely sensitive situation. If we are to continue, and there is no technical reason why we shouldn't, we are keen to know the views of every participating country and to discuss any extra safeguards we can put in place so as not to hinder the MCA's investigation. As you know, all the safety cases for this exercise were verified previously, but they will be under further scrutiny now. So you are being asked to review your on board ship procedures to confirm that nothing could have happened that could cause concern with the authorities. We will be doing the same. It shouldn't take long, but the Exercise will only continue once we can demonstrate full compliance to our safety case and each participating nation is content to proceed."

Matt was disappointed that the emphasis was not more on understanding what had happened and chasing the authorities for the actual cause of death, rather than just clearing their name. But he guessed that Mike wouldn't see that as his problem. Several muttered conversations had broken out around the table. Skip sat back, looking at the floor. He and other members of the Range team were visibly upset. Mike called the meeting to order. "I will now open the floor to discussion."

Not surprisingly, it was Bob Halifax who responded first. He cleared his throat and scratched his beard as he began.

"Ehm, on behalf of Her Majesty's government, the UK Ministry of Defence and indeed the Royal Navy, I would firstly like to thank the Hebrides Range for your diligent work. I absolutely agree with you that I cannot begin to perceive how our activities could have any connection to whatever is going on. In my thirty years at sea I have never seen the like and I am sure none of you have either."

Not that they would admit to it if they had, thought Matt.

Bob shook his head sorrowfully, more for their reputation than for the environmental disaster.

"Personally I think it would be a shame to stop as we were doing so well, but I do however concur with the Range's approach and would welcome the views of our international colleagues."

The French and Dutch both thanked Mike politely for his brief and assured him that they agreed that it was an "Off Range issue". Matt didn't like the way the carnage he saw was being minimised, but he needed to wait to snare the culprit. In respect of local sensitivities, they continued, they would of course review procedures and consult with their respective ministries before formally agreeing to proceed. Mike nodded in agreement; this was the response and support he was hoping for. Skip was still looking down.

Mike turned to the senior American officer, Hank, to invite his view. Hank didn't look up initially; he was fiddling with some papers in front of him. Finally, he spoke.

"I have a statement from my government." He looked around the room with his chin jutting belligerently out in righteous indignation. He read aloud; "The United States government does not wish to be part of any activity that could potentially be causing such environmental damage. We have been utilising the Russian system. It is not, to our mind, independently proven to be safe, therefore cannot be considered so. Therefore, we have no option but to withdraw."

Everyone in the room was stunned. Undeterred, Hank stared Mike straight in the eyes and continued:

"Our intelligence indicates that Russian infiltrators have been assisted by Range staff, either unwittingly or on purpose, to undermine this exercise and gather intelligence. This is not a situation we are prepared to allow to continue."

"Your intelligence?" It was Skip, who now sat bolt upright glaring across the room. The atmosphere was electric, nobody dared breathe. "When were you going to share this "intelligence" with us, pray tell?" Despite being at the other side of the room, the question slammed down on the American.

Flippantly Wally shrugged. "Not everyone here meets our standard of security clearance, so we are not in a position to elaborate, even if we wanted to."

Several throats were cleared around the room. Skip's eyebrows had risen above where his hairline used to be. Boris was purple with rage, he jumped to his feet, leaned across the table and waved his arms and shouted rapidly in Russian. He gesticulated wildly, prodding the air in the direction of Wally and Hank.

Skip was also on his feet now, trying to regain control of the meeting. Ivan, more collected, rested his arm on his colleague's shoulder and pushed him back into his seat. He caught Skip's eye. "I must insist that I speak, not only to refute the horrendous statement just made, but to give the viewpoint of the Russian Government."

Skip nodded his assent, the Americans muttered to each other under their breath.

Ivan continued. "The Russian government is also very unhappy about the environmental occurrences, and give our condolences to the local fishermen. We understand the difficulties this type of vandalism could cause the working man."

Wally snorted derisively. Ivan ignored him.

"We believe that somebody has been tampering with the Russian equipment in order to discredit our participation, in a cynical act of, as I said, vandalism. We have not been spying on our comrades here. Our concern has been to achieve the objectives of this exercise. However, we surmise the only people who have had access to do this are the imperialists opposite, either directly or by duping gullible members of our host's staff. The Russian Government formally requests that their actions are investigated thoroughly by an independent third party, in the meantime we have been instructed to leave and have no further part of this."

As Ivan finished, folding a piece of paper in front of him, Skip had difficulty holding the meeting together. He tried to say that while he appreciated the super powers were so concerned about the local fish, he would need them to provide their evidence separately to him, but nobody was listening. Anxious exchanges were taking place across the room. Matt looked around. Alex was white, staring fixedly ahead. Frank was surveying the room too, looking on edge and alertly taking everything in. Carl looked wired. Matt caught his eye and nodded imperceptibly towards everyone else in the room, but the boy was ready.

Like a man possessed, Carl jumped to his feet. "I am so sick of this. You are all bloody just, just ... at it! Let's stop this right here and start talking straight. It's me you are all calling gullible, unwitting, well, I have something to say. None of you give a shit about the fish, and you..." He swung round to Mike, "You don't give a shit about me either!"

"Sit down and be quiet, or I will ask you to leave," barked a red-faced Mike.

"No way, you heard them, now you'll hear me and I haven't even started yet. Who was gullible? I told you all something was wrong, but nobody believed me." He thumped the table then turned on Wally. "As for you, you lanky waste of oxygen, you accused me of incompetence; you wouldn't know if I was or wasn't, you were too busy catching your own ugly reflection to know what was going on. Either give us the evidence that I screwed up the readings or give me a full apology for calling me a liar now, before I make an official complaint!"

Hank was aghast. Ivan and Boris were laughing, lapping this up. But Carl wasn't finished. He turned to face them. "Aye, you understand me alright now do you? You refused to speak English to us, complained when I spoke my own language in my own country, didn't even manage to spell my name right when you complained about me. You understand now though don't you?" He muttered something insulting in Gaelic. "God knows what you were programming that thing to do. I don't know what you were doing, but you were up to no good. I don't need to speak Russian to know that."

Both Russians were on their feet, shouting at Carl in Russian.

"Enough's enough," muttered Mike. "Get him out of here."

From the corner of his eye Carl could see two of his colleagues moving purposefully towards him. "You just don't get it do you?" He looked around desperately. Along the centre of the table there were large jugs of water. He grinned deviously as he grabbed one in each hand and aimed the contents to drench first the Americans and then the Russians. There was uproar. He didn't resist as two sets of hands grabbed him firmly by the shoulders. He was paying no attention and seemed remarkably calm despite the various people shouting at him.

The room calmed down as Carl was escorted out of the room. Mike was apologising profusely to anyone who would listen. People were passing the Americans and Russians tissues to help them dry themselves down. It was when Ivan turned to thank someone, that he noticed the two empty seats. He yelled at Boris..."она ушла! быстро найти!"

Boris took only a split second to scan the room and then started pushing chairs out of his way, like an ungainly rhinoceros, as he charged round the table towards the door. He was almost out, with Ivan still shouting behind him, when Frank inexplicably turned around and stretched his legs. The Russian went flying into the water cooler with a clatter of swearing and spinning chairs.

"What on earth is going on?" Skip demanded.

Mike was glaring as he helped the disgruntled Russian to his feet. They were joined immediately by Ivan. He did not assist his colleague, but walked straight past him into the corridor. Boris's head was cut. Skip wasn't sure what was happening either, but decided it was best not to let him go anywhere. People were milling about. Bob Halifax's face had become puce. He was shaking his head and apologising to people. He was assuring any one that would listen that "the boy" would be dealt with. He was regretting the fact that as a civilian, he could not be court martialled. Mike adjourned the meeting, but he was only stating the obvious, the meeting was most definitely over. After a few moments Ivan returned. He spoke to Boris tersely in their native tongue before addressing Mike.

"We are very concerned Dr. Alex is missing. She would not have left voluntarily. We are concerned for her wellbeing. We are afraid she may have been taken off the site against her will."

Mike finally lost his poise and rolled his eyes at Skip. "I am sure she hasn't gone far," was what he managed to say. Skip asked a female member of staff to check the "ladies room".

"I have done that already," muttered Ivan.

"What do you want us to do then?" retorted Skip.

The Russian paused, then looked him straight in the eye.

"You have a camera at the gate. I would like to see the CCTV footage of the cars that have left in the last few minutes. Can I do that? She is very important to us."

Mike wasn't sure, but Bob was insisting that he should do everything he could to assist.

"This is most irregular...I am not sure...." He worried. But Skip was more pragmatic.

"C'mon, let's just get this over and done with quickly. I can even tell you if she has used her pass to swipe out. Follow me." The Russian looked confused.

"Let's see if she has actually left the site." Skip called over his shoulder as he left the room.

Mike was uneasy. According to the rules, permission should have been sought and given, before allowing a foreign national to view Range security footage; however, he appreciated the need to calm the atmosphere and put these paranoid notions to rest; so he went along.

Frank, Bob, Skip and Mike crowded into the cramped reception area with their Russian visitors. The Americans left in disgust muttering about wanting no part of further irregularities pandering to the enemy. Skip firstly logged onto the guards' workstation and pulled up a multi-coloured chart. "According to this, she is still on site. Well, at least her pass is. But let's scroll through the footage."

Skip wasn't really worried as he was happy that the Range had nothing to hide. He was proven correct as there was no sign so far of the Russian doctor passing through the gates in any vehicle. Frank held his breath as a grainy image of Matt's car approached the camera. But all that could be seen was the solitary figure of Matt driving, giving the camera a cheery wave as he left.

As the Russians left reception to continue their search for Alex, the senior Range staff were shell shocked, aware that events were spinning out of control around them, but not sure how to stop them. "You need to get Carl back and we need to talk," said Frank.

"This had better be good. Or there is going to be hell to pay," muttered Mike.

~~~~~~~~~~~~~~~~~~~~~~~~~

Chapter Fourteen: Gone Fishing

Matt felt strangely relaxed as he drove 'up south' to meet with Stuart. He knew they had work to do, but the morning had gone well so far. He felt oddly optimistic. The morning weather too had calmed down as he drove along the single track coast road. The sea looked almost inviting. It reminded him of a turquoise crushed velvet blanket that he would soon be wrapped in. Bring it on, he thought, I'm ready.

Once a decent distance from the Range, Matt pulled over in a passing place. He got out and stretched, enjoying the warmth of the autumn sun on his back. He leisurely strolled to the back of his car and opened the boot.

"Good morning professor. Would you like me to help you out of there?" He offered his hand and helped Alex clamber out. She straightened her clothing and ran her fingers through her hair.

"Are we going to meet the boat again?" She asked as she climbed into the car. "I don't have any paperwork, no passport or documents, Boris took them from me."

Matt assured her that she would not need any. He explained that they would be going by boat again, but this time they would be travelling in a fishing boat rather than the RIB. He had started driving south again. The boat was moored at Lochboisdale harbour. They just needed to get on board and she would be hidden below deck. Alex stared out of the window, chewing at her nails, obviously still worried about something. Matt was trying to work out how to break the rest of his plan to her but she interrupted his train of thought.

"I see how there is more shelter and fishing boat is a good disguise, but is it not slower than the RIB? We will have to move quickly. They have a warship out there and now they will be looking for me."

"Yes, but that's just it. We are not going to be running from them. We are going to be exactly where they would be going if you hadn't complicated their plans and we are going to wait for them. We will catch them at the scene of their crimes here in Scotland, so get them out of the way and keep them busy while you can make your case against them and the University."

Alex had turned in her seat and was staring at him in shock.

"Are you mad? This is still about the fish isn't it? They don't care about that. They are international killers. We will all end up dead and be thrown in the ocean where no one will find us. Then, more people will die because nobody will stop them."

"It's not about fish; it's not about politics either. It's about good or indeed bad old fashioned theft. I tracked your ROVs movements last night. They think there is treasure or something buried at sea and have been searching for it. We will catch them in the act of trying to retrieve it. Then we discredit...."

"Discredit them? These people don't care about being discredited! This is far too risky, too dangerous."

Alex sat back in her seat, twisting her back to Matt, she folded her arms and glared out of the window.

"Listen to me. I will get you back to the mainland and to safety. I promise. Of course I care about the fish and I don't want them to get away with it, but it is more than that. If we just go, they will have alerted their people and there will be another Boris and Ivan waiting for us as soon as we step ashore. In the city you won't know what they look like or where they will be coming from; how will you be safe then? You will be looking over your shoulder, worried about every stranger. Believe me, it is not a good way to live. This way, they have been caught by their own greed and by stopping them for an environmental incident it means that whoever they are working for at your University is less likely to be covering his tracks against your allegations. You will be safer."

Alex was listening now, but still didn't seem convinced.

"Look, back-up is on its way. The Range will be calling the authorities by now. Stuart is going to pretend to be fishing as a decoy. You will be hidden the whole time. All we are doing is delaying them until help arrives. It is better for you in the long run."

"They would kill a fisherman if they thought he was getting in their way." She objected, but with far less enthusiasm. She's getting it, thought Matt as turned back around and she was at least prepared, if not happy, to go along with him. She had little choice. He decided not to tell her that the "back up" would be arriving only if Skip could be persuaded to believe rather than arrest Carl and that he was not sure who would actually be turning up to find the ancient gold.

They sat in silence as the car turned off the main road in Lochboisdale to head for the harbour. From the north end of the village Alex couldn't actually see the pontoons or boats. It had been dark the last time she had been here, so she hadn't noticed how the masts only became apparent as you travelled over the long causeway that connected the breakwaters and quayside to the mainland. They parked and walked quickly across the quayside to the pontoon bridge that led to the boats. There was an array of small vessels tied up, the Marine Harvest "well boats" and small fishing boats with brightly coloured cabins and assorted equipment dangling over the sides. It was a peaceful scene of everyday normality as their reflections gleamed in the sheltered waters. There was no one about. It seemed impossible to believe that only a few miles away there was such environmental devastation and the impending threat to life and limb. Alex followed Matt along the pontoon walk way. He was heading toward the end of the pontoons. As they were halfway along a man that Alex didn't recognise came out of one of the boats and waved. Matt must have heard her intake of breath. "That's Paul, Stuart's brother. It is his boat we are taking."

They climbed aboard. The boat was called the Lady Mary. It was yellow and white, twenty feet long, with a small cabin and cluttered deck. Inside there were side benches, a small central table and a tiny stove. There was a little door leading off to a miniscule wheelhouse that comprised of a small bunk, gas burner and kit cupboard. The stern was piled high with creels.

"He's made me clean up for the lassie coming aboard," smiled Paul, as he handed them both mugs of steaming tea and Stuart emerged from the wheelhouse. "Thought you'd want this before you head off."

Stuart wasn't so jovial, he hadn't told his brother the full story, he did not want to admit how scared he actually felt. Matt rummaged in his pocket and handed him a piece of paper.

"Aye, that's where I thought we'd be heading. It was a pitiful sight this morning".

As they drank their tea, squashed into the small cabin, Matt told them about what he and Carl had discussed the night before. They remembered tales of shipwrecks and sea monsters from when they were children, but no one ever really believed them.

They agreed their plan of action. Stuart started to get himself ready. "Aye, well this is real enough, I've sent some fish, seaweed and water samples off to SAMS, but had no result as yet, but maybe in a couple of hours we will be able to tell them what it is all about."

Paul was going to leave them and drive Matt's car away. They exchanged phone numbers and details of which people to ring just in case things went wrong. Matt wanted to ensure that he had several back up plans in place. He didn't say it, but he agreed with Alex, that they would be dealing with desperate ruthless people and he had no intention of being a hero.

On the journey Matt and Alex stayed in the cabin out of sight. They knew what time the treasure hunters planned to be there and had timed their trip to arrive about an hour before. They were on schedule as Stuart stopped the boat and dropped anchor about a mile and a half off shore. Stuart could see the rocky east coast of Uist, which he had known from boyhood, the green lump of Stuley Island just to the north, where he had helped to shear sheep in

151

summers gone by, but it was not the same. They were surrounded by the sea, the gigantic sky and the ominous silence of the remaining stunned and dead animals from the previous night's activities. Although there were far fewer corpses than earlier every other living being seemed to have deserted the area too including the sea eagles which he knew nested on the cliffs a short distance away. Perhaps they too were unnerved by whatever and whoever was about to come over the horizon. He turned the radio on as a distraction.

"This is so creepy," he said aloud. "I hope they turn up soon. I won't need much of an excuse to wallop someone."

"Stick to the plan," Matt reminded him from his hiding place below. These are dangerous people. You can't provoke them. Just stall them." Matt was still working on the premise that they would not want to kill a random local as he hoped they would think it might blow their cover and chances of escape.

As they had planned, Stuart started throwing his creels over the side. They trailed in a fleet behind the small boat. He set and lifted them partly to pass the time, but also to look realistic to any potential company. They were heavy and clumsy and there were a lot of them. He stopped and surveyed the horizon.

"I tell you Macaulay, this had better work. I hope you are enjoying sitting watching me do all the hard labour. If I lose these creels I'll be sending you the bill."

"Exercise will do you good," responded Matt. The banter broke the tension and helped with the nerves.

"There's only us about for miles. This could be a long morning. You really think we will be joined by other boats? Where are they going to get them from? I'll know most of the boats from round here."

That was a good question, thought Matt. "If they are military, they'll have removed a landing craft of some sort from one of the support ships in the exercise. It will depend on how much top cover they have or whether they are working alone. We will have to wait and see."

He pottered round the boat for a further fifteen minutes, then looking south, Stuart spoke without turning round. "We have company. Looks like a little speed boat with two people on board. It's not local, so must be military. Rate it's going at; it will be here soon. It's show time, I hope you two are out of sight. I also hope their Gaelic is better than my Russian".

As they got closer, still looking forward, Stuart described what he saw to Matt.

"There are two men... It looks like they are in military uniform. One looks like a washed out country and western singer, the other like Buzz Lightyear, you know, big jaw and shoulders but no hips."

He did not want to use his binoculars, or even appear too interested, but as they approached he got a better view of what they had on board. "Surprise, surprise, it looks like they have diving gear piled up on the back of that boat. D'you know I think they have wet suits on under those uniform jackets too. They don't look pleased to see me... Ah, isn't that nice, they are smiling and waving. Think he has a loud hailer, probably doesn't know how to use the ship to ship communications."

"Good morning Sir," came the unexpectedly polite salutation. "I am a representative of the United States Government acting on behalf of Her Majesty the Queen of England. We are investigating this terrible environmental problem and have to take some water samples here. I am therefore instructing you to lift your anchor and move away."

"Aye right," retorted Stuart loudly. There was a pause. "That disnae sound like Russian to me," he said more quietly.

Down below, Matt and Alex stared at each other. This was not what they had expected. "Should we go up?" mouthed Alex.

Matt shook his head. "Let's just stick to the plan."

The American couldn't make out what Stuart had said so hailed again. He repeated his introduction, adding "I don't know if you heard me the first time but I must insist you move your vessel immediately."

Stuart didn't say anything. He picked up the hand set from his intercom system and waved it at the other boat. "Jeeze," he muttered when they didn't respond. He pointed at it and held it to his ear. It took a few seconds for the American to catch on, but a moment later his comms system crackled.

It was Wally's voice which came through the speaker. He repeated his message.

"Yeah, yeah, I got all that." Stuart had to contain himself, he wanted to swear at them and tell them what he really thought, but he knew it was down to him alone to keep them here so that they could be apprehended.

"Well, about time too. I was wondering when you guys would take responsibility for your actions. I am so glad you're here. We are really worried about what is going on, this is really terrible you know. What can I do to help?"

"Move." was the monosyllabic reply. Stuart could see Wally was working hard to keep the genial smile on his face.

"Well, you know I really would love to help. The only the thing is I have just put down all my creels. I can't just move them away. It will be really dangerous for me to bring them in too quickly. Don't want to capsize or snare them and delay you in any way. Maybe I could take the water samples for you?"

Stuart shrugged and tried to look apologetic. He watched and waited while the Americans conferred.

Wally sounded firmer. "We haven't got time for that, just bring them in, or we will get rid of them for you."

Stuart drew himself up to his full height. The Americans had brought their boat closer. He could now stare them in the eye.

"Now hold the bus, don't you think that talk like that is just a bit hasty and not very polite. It's my waters you have contaminated here." He paused and looked from one to the other.

"Now let's see, I have just put down fifteen creels. They cost about £50.00 each. So If they got damaged I'd lose... " he paused again, feigning the calculation in his head. "Seven hundred and fifty pounds. Plus, the value of the catch. I can't afford to lose that, pal. On top of that, it will take me weeks to order and replace them; think of how much earnings I would lose then. I would need compensation."

Again the Americans conferred hastily. They were obviously not happy. From what Stuart could hear, they were debating whether they should insist or come back later. They were looking at their watches. It seemed they had some time pressure or deadline to keep themselves.

It was Hank this time who responded. "Ok that's fine, because this is so important to all of us, we will authorise compensation on this occasion. Now can you just get on with it." He was trying to sound in command but the pitch of his voice gave away his anxiety.

Realising they were in a hurry Stuart waited, he wasn't going to be rushed. He rubbed his chin. "Hmm. Well thanks. That's perfect, but the thing is though, I can't just turn up at the rocket Range with a bill saying some bloke I met at sea said it would be OK to get paid now, can I?" He paused again. Scrunched his brow and then smiled as if he just had a good idea. "I know what, either you could come closer and give me a written guarantee or I could ring the Range and just ask them to confirm. Will only take a minute, what d'you you think? I think I have the switchboard number or is there someone specific I should ask for?" he rummaged for his mobile phone and held it up triumphantly.

"Don't push too much," hissed Matt.

But Wally didn't need that much pushing; he was seeing his dreams slip away from him. He couldn't believe his fortune was being denied from him by some stupid red neck local.

He cursed the fact that he didn't have his gun to hand but grabbed the next best thing and closer to hand. Aiming a flare gun at Stuart's boat, his large chin quivering, he made himself uncompromisingly clear.

"You move that pile of junk now, or I will blow a hole in it so big that you will be swimming home dragging your soggy crap behind you. Now get the fuck out of here!"

Hank came forward and put his hand on Wally's shoulder to try and bring some calm to the situation, but neither man could understand why Stuart did not respond or seem worried; he was simply standing grinning at them.

Stuart was looking past them. At what appeared to be a speedboat heading purposefully in their direction.

"Well that is an interesting suggestion," he said lazily. "I might've been feart, but as they say down your way, looks like the cavalry have arrived and just in time." The two Americans glanced quickly behind them. "Put that right out of the way," Hank snapped at Wally. "We have no problem here. We are just trying to help, remember. Nobody else knows what's down there apart from the fish."

Matt, who had been listening behind the cabin door, began to open it slowly.

"Hang on Ma tha," muttered Stuart. "Something's not right". He picked up his binoculars to get a better view.

"What is it?" Matt had the door open, he had to strain to hear as Stuart was talking quietly and still had his back to him.

Stuart was scanning the sea with his binoculars. "Well, I'm not sure, 'cos I've only really seen this sort of thing on films, but it really looks like the approaching boat, which is not one

I recognise, has some sort of gun mounting... a tripod anyway, with something on it and a bloke standing behind it. The writing on the side looks foreign. I don't like this Matt."

Alex became agitated. Matt tried, as quietly as he could to calm her down. "We must go now. It must be Boris and Ivan... we must leave now." She was half whispering and half sobbing. She was very scared.

"I can hear you..." muttered Stuart in a sing song voice.

Hank who had been watching the approaching vessel, now turned back towards the Lady Mary.

"What did you say?"
"Nothing, mate, just wondering what the hell is going on. What's a guy gotta do just to get a bit of fishing?" he started noisily clomping around the boat.

He decided to maintain the pretence and continued talking to himself. To the Americans it sounded as if he was moaning to himself in Gaelic. He was actually giving Matt a description of what he could see.

Matt took Alex by the shoulders and whispered as quietly as he could. "Now listen. As you said earlier, we can't outrun them and we have nothing to match any type of mounted gun. Let's see if Stuart can talk us out of here, he is, after all, just an innocent bystander. If he can't bluff them, we will have to take our chances. Leave them to argue for a minute. If they are looking for you they will think you are with the yanks. Not on here."

Alex was not convinced; she knew how ruthless Boris and Ivan could be when people got in their way. She took a deep breath, closed her eyes and made herself as small as possible. She felt Matt squeeze her shoulder, she wished she could feel as confident as he did.

As the speedboat pulled up the other two vessels swayed in its wake. Stuart did not recognise the two men on board but Hank & Wally obviously did. They were not intimidated by the sight of the gun, more furious at the interruption. Hank stepped towards them. He addressed the new arrivals with a belligerent tone. "What are you doing here, come to see the damage you have caused?"

The Russians were not to be put off. "We are here to rescue our comrade that you have kidnapped. Hand her over now."

Hank and Wally were genuinely confused. "What is this bullshit?" exclaimed Wally waving his arms in the air. "What hostage? Do we look like we have a hostage?" He wanted to cry, this was beyond belief. He could not believe another distraction was getting between him and his destiny.

"I am deadly serious," barked Ivan. "If you do not give her up I will board your boat to search for her. Be in no doubt that any resistance will be met with deadly force."

"The United States Government would consider that an act of war," blustered Hank. He sounded a little less confident. "We have absolutely no interest or idea where your colleague is."

"Time to go," muttered Stuart as he moved as silently as he could around the boat. He started to flip the switch to automatically release his lobster creels, but turned it off concerned that its electronic motor on the hauler would attract their attention. Instead he silently used his knife to slash the ropes and reluctantly let his creels float away.

Stuart moved back into his cabin. "Just going to try to quietly sidle out of range," he muttered in Gaelic. He gently raised his anchor then released the clutch. He waited a few moments then quietly put his boat into gear. The Lady Mary started to edge away from the other boats unnoticed. Could this work?

Suddenly and inexplicably the Lady Mary's engine coughed. As if noticing them for the first time Boris swung his gun directly towards Stuart. "Stop!"

Every nerve in Stuart's brain was screaming. He took a deep breath, he had to stay calm, he was very aware that all their lives could depend on what he said next. He sounded far more nonchalant than he felt. "Hey man, I have nothing to do with this. Don't tell me what to do. I was just using the momentum of my boat to balance my creels. I don't give a monkeys what you guys are up to. I take it that this is part of your exercise thing that's happening. To be honest, I'm pissed off about the whole thing, I don't like you closing off the fishing areas. All I'm trying to do is earn my living out of your way and these idiots come along and start threatening me. I agree with you; I think they're up to something too. I was going to complain, but if it gets you all out of my way any quicker, I guess I'll just go and leave you guys to it. OK Ma tha?"

The Russians conversed rapidly. Stuart was somewhat relieved to see the gun lowered slightly.

Ivan addressed him in a slightly more civil tone. He still wanted to maintain control of the situation. "Yes, yes, this is just part of the exercise. It is a search and rescue test. However, participants are allowed to enlist native help when needed, so I must check because they might have transferred their prisoner to your boat. We will search them first, then you." His tone hardened. "But if you do try and move your boat again we will shoot. Do you understand?"

"No shit, some exercise," sighed Stuart. "We'll see about that. Native help indeed!" He turned his back on them and defiantly spat over the side of the boat. He sat on the gunwale and took his phone out of his pocket. He had no signal. He leaned back, folded his arms.

"I do hope you got a plan Macaulay, cos I'm all out of ideas."

~~~~~~~~~~~~~~~~~~~~~~~~~~~~~~

Chapter Fifteen: Telling the tale

Back on the Range, Carl was worried. He was in the dog house again for his outburst at the morning meeting but that was not what was preying on his mind. Matt had given him one last instruction. If he hadn't heard from Matt within four hours he was to raise the alarm. He had hoped that he would know who the mystery ROV operator was because he thought that they would have left just after Matt and the Russian woman, but he didn't get a chance to see because he had been taken directly to the guard room and left in an empty office behind reception. He had been told to stay there, "or else".

Carl wanted to be able to tell Skip and Mike who the culprits were, he thought that it would have given his story at least some credibility. But that hadn't worked, because as far as he could hear both of the involved parties had hung around on site. He had even heard the Russians in reception with Mike. It sounded as if the Director was letting them see who had left the site, which was odd. He was sure he heard them say something about Matt being in a car by himself, which was also worrying. Did it mean that the Americans had the woman? It was three and a half hours later and he had no way of contacting Matt. He hoped that Matt had been able to talk to Frank, surely at least that would make things a bit easier. He didn't like the thought that Matt could be in danger and he was the only person who knew about it.

It was Frank who finally came to see him. He told him that the Director wanted to talk with both of them. He confirmed that he had spoken briefly with Matt, who had vouched for Carl, but he warned that Mike would take some convincing, so he had better have his facts straight. This was not going to be easy.

Carl felt like a condemned man as he followed Frank along the corridor. People were giving him sideways glances then looking away. Nobody was talking or making eye contact. If the atmosphere was cool in the corridor, it became positively icy when they entered the

Director's office. Mike sat at his desk, Skip stood beside him. Their expressions were grim. The door was shut behind them. Carl and Frank were not invited to sit down.

Mike cleared his throat, looked from one to the other, then just shook his head. He was lost for words. "I don't quite know where to start," he admitted. "You both know how important this exercise is to us and indeed the whole of the country." He looked directly at Carl. "I have never, ever, seen such an irresponsible, stupid display such as yours this morning. Do you have any idea just how much worse you have made an already very serious situation?"

Despite knowing, he had an explanation, Carl withered under his glare.

"If that wasn't bad enough," Mike continued. "I am told that there is evidence that the control room communication feeds have been tampered with. If you have had anything at all to do with this, you will not just be fired, but you could be looking at a lengthy prison sentence. Espionage is taken very seriously by both our own and the American governments. I wouldn't be able to help you, even if I wanted to. Which at this point in time, believe me, is highly unlikely."

Carl shuffled from one foot to another. He opened his mouth to speak, but Mike raised his hand. He had not finished. He turned his attention to Frank.

"As for you... While he is just stupid, I really expected better from you. Are you just so incredibly clumsy or did you have some sort of mental aberration? Skip tells me you claim to have an explanation. What I want to know is what on earth made you think that you had the right to take unilateral violent action towards an international guest on my Range? I can't wait to hear it."

Mike folded his arms and sat down, waiving his hands dismissively indication that the others could sit too. Frank had his head down and his eyes shut. He was not used to being spoken to in this way. Perhaps he had been a bit rash in flooring the Russian, he thought. He hoped that Mike would share his faith in Matt's explanation. In a quiet voice he repeated his conversation with Matt that morning. Skip and Mike exchanged glances, but did not interrupt him. Mike scribbled the odd note on the paper in front of him.

"I don't know what his full brief was." Frank concluded. "He did imply that he had used our systems to gain information. I don't know how, but he did say that he would take full responsibility for the hacking or whatever it is that has happened to our IT system. He didn't want Carl to be blamed for it."

"I hardly think that's his call," muttered Mike. He was definitely not convinced. He felt undermined. His annoyance shifted to those he felt had damaged his chain of command. "I can't believe that whoever it is that Matt is supposedly working for didn't deign to keep me informed... but then again... This is just not good enough!"

Skip was more intrigued. He had known Matt since he was a boy and trusted him. He had been at Carl's christening; he had watched him grow up. The boy was bright; he found it hard to believe that he would recklessly cause an international incident. "I think we should hear what Carl has to say," he suggested.

Mike didn't look enthusiastic, but reluctantly agreed. "Go on then, we have to get to the bottom of this before anything else happens and I have to work out what on earth I am going to put in my report."

Faltering at first, Carl started to tell his tale. He was careful to keep everything in chronological order and to include the information and instructions Matt had given him. He showed them the crumpled version of the poem that he still had in his pocket, and described what they had witnessed overnight. Like Frank, he didn't understand why Alex was in danger, but on another scrunched up piece of paper he had the co-ordinates of where Matt had been heading in the Lady Mary.

Mike found it all hard to believe. "This is beyond ridiculous."

162

"He didn't mention a ship wreck or any of this to me," agreed Frank.

"I think he was more worried about Alex this morning," offered Carl. "I know what you're thinking; we couldn't believe it either when we saw it."

Skip, on the other hand, was not so sceptical. "Local folklore is full of stories of shipwrecks off our coasts." He was quite animated. He brought out sea charts and started mapping out the co-ordinates that Carl had given them. He poured over the map, making calculations; he agreed that the timings would work. "Any sunken treasure would of course be the property of the Scottish Government," he mused.

Carl was relieved that he was finally being believed, but was still conscious of time passing. "The thing is, we still haven't heard from Matt. He could be in trouble."

Mike had become a little more relaxed. Maybe too relaxed for Carl's liking.

"I don't see this as a Range matter."

Carl felt sick, they couldn't abandon Matt now.

"No, the more I think about it. Yes it is theft, but it is not in Range waters and Matt and the Russian scientist, who has chosen to go with him, are not after all Range employees. This isn't a Range matter; I think we should talk to the police."

Carl didn't care as long as they got on with it. It was over four hours now. He suddenly remembered another point that Matt had mentioned.

"Matt said that if I didn't hear from him and if you guys didn't believe me... I had to contact Inspector MacRury and to ask her to contact a man called Murdo MacNeil... whoever he is."

Inspector Florence Macrury was in her office pondering over the lasts week's events. She was a small, well built woman in her forties, with auburn hair cut into a short bob. She liked to be smart and for everything to be in order. Even alone in her office she wore her uniform with style and poise.

She was reading the station log for the previous week and felt perplexed. Every now and again things got a little more exciting when there was an exercise taking place on the rocket Range, but it usually never amounted to much more than a squabble over some lassie or some poor unfortunate ending in a ditch because they were not used to the single track roads and passing places. But this was different. She wondered what the link was between the fireworks behind the post office and the vandalised car, that could have been the local neds but the uproar at the stables and upsetting the horses seemed out of character even for them: she would have to step up patrols. Thinking of animals her mind wandered to the problem up south, of the dead and stunned fish, which was even more bizarre.

The vets were trying to work out if that was some sort of environmental protest or old fashioned pollution. The Harbour Master had called an emergency meeting. She had been asked to report on the likelihood of it being some sort of criminal activity or vandalism. Highly unlikely, she thought. What would anyone have to gain? There had been cases in the past of people using explosives to blast fish out of the water as a cruel and lazy way to fish, but there was no evidence of that here.

Her thoughts were interrupted by the sharp ring of the phone on the edge of her desk.

It was reception. "Sorry to bother you Ma'am, Frank Miller is here and is requesting to see you urgently."

"Is he in the diary? Can't you deal with it?" She liked Frank and would normally make time for him, but she really did need to prepare for this meeting.

"No Ma'am, he insists on seeing you."

"Then fit him in for the first appointment then, tell him I am sorry, but I really am busy right now."

There was a pause. Florence was about to hang up, but she could hear Frank persisting on the other end of the line. There was another person there too.

"He says it is very urgent. He needs you to contact a... Murdo MacNeil. It's with regards to..." The PC was about to ask Frank to confirm the second name he had mentioned, but Florence was able to tell her who it was. "Matt Macaulay?"

"Yes Ma'am."

She sighed. There went the paperwork. "Send them in."

She had heard that Matt had some sort of government job that took him back and forth to the mainland and had wondered if it was to do with Murdo. Could this explain some of the strange things that had been happening? On their past history, Matt and Murdo being involved certainly changed things.

Even though it was half open, there was a tentative knock on her door. "Come in, come in," she called. She waved her hand expansively, "pull up a chair and tell me why you want to bother such a high heid yin as Mr. MacNeil?"

Two men entered her office. Neither man smiled as they both sat down. She noticed how strained they both looked. The young man with Frank looked absolutely drained. She couldn't place him, but he certainly seemed agitated and obviously had a lot on his mind. Frank introduced Carl. Yes of course, the Macphee boy.

"I hear you're quite a footballer," she said, trying to calm him, but he still did not smile. He had his phone in his hand and was hardly taking his eyes off it, as if willing it to ring. He was either pushed for time, or waiting for a call.

"You better tell me what's so urgent then?" She looked from one to the other.

Once again Carl told his story. This time it was with a little more urgency, he was worried that they were wasting time. He was also aware of just how bizarre he sounded and was concerned that the policewoman would not believe him, or start asking lots of questions. He didn't have maps or the timings with him to verify anything. Florence just listened; she doodled abstractly on her notepad as he spoke. When Carl had finished she nodded and thought for a moment. She then asked him to confirm how long it had been since he had last heard from Matt.

"OK," she replied, "We better make the call." She opened a drawer in her desk, rummaged through some papers then took out a business card. She looked at it, straightened it and then holding it with one hand she dialled the number shown with the other.

"Murdo, it's Florence, yes, Florence Macrury from Benbecula." She smiled at whatever it was he said. She unconsciously ran her fingers through her hair and removed a nonexistent piece of fluff from the front of her jacket. She gave a brief summary of Carl's information. The voice on the end of the phone did not seem surprised; it was almost as if he had been expecting the call. She listened. He was obviously giving her some sort of background brief.

"Well we do think we know where they are, but we have not heard from them in a while."

"-So would you like me to save your bacon again?" she said cheekily. "That will cost you another dinner."

Carl and Frank exchanged glances, what was going on?

She became serious again. "And that is your priority?"

"-Well, I will see what I can do."

She listened again.

"Yes, yes, of course. I will keep you informed and send your prodigal child home, yes." She looked at her watch. "Fine, no problem, bye, bye, bye now." She was in a rush now to get off the line.

Frank and Carl were expecting and hoping for an explanation of the conversation they had just heard, but none was forthcoming. Instead the Inspector picked up the phone again and speaking to the PC on reception she asked him to find her the short wave contact number of the Lady Mary and to bring it through immediately.

She then turned to Carl and Frank. "I am going to talk to them, and try to get them to bring whatever is happening closer to the shore. We can't deal with it while they are out on the water."

There was a knock on the door and the PC came in with a post it note, with a phone number written on it. Florence thanked him then told him to contact everyone. "I do mean everyone mind, leave is cancelled and I am afraid you'll have to get yesterday's night shift out of bed too. Tell them to be on standby to come in. I will give you a rendezvous point as soon as I have it, but get them prepared."

"Shall I inform Inverness Ma'am?"

"No thanks, we don't have time to wait. I'll do that in a bit... I have authority to proceed."

When the constable had left, she gave a tight smile to Carl and Frank. "Ok, Ma tha, here goes. We'll use the conference phone; you can listen but you must stay quiet. Do you understand?"

They sat up quickly. Carl just wanted to get on with it.

Finally, Florence dialled the number. A crackle echoed around the room. Then it rang and rang and rang.

Chapter Sixteen: All at sea

Stuart Steele was trying his best to stay calm.

Matt had come out of the wheel house and was sitting on the floor in the cabin so that he could hear better what was going on.

"Play along and buy some time." Matt whispered to him. "Make him think you have nothing to hide here. Pretend that you can't understand him. Be cool and friendly whatever he says. He has to think you have nothing to worry about."

"Aye right," muttered Stuart; he was not feeling so brave.

"Try and divert attention away from us. C'mon you can do it. I'm gonna try and hide Alex in that old waterproof store at the end of the cabin. So if they do have a quick look below they might not see her. They will be more shocked at seeing me. We'll say, like them, I didn't trust the yanks, so got you to bring me out to see what they are up to. We have no choice Ma tha."

Suddenly a light started flashing on Stuart's console. "It's the short wave radio" he muttered to Matt. "Who the heck would be calling us now?"

"Can you answer it without being obvious?"
"No, but you can, hang on."
Stuart stepped into the cabin of the boat. He leaned forward, looking through the windscreen at the other vessels. Without looking down he knocked the radio handset to the floor towards Matt. He pressed the respond button on the dashboard.

The occupants of the two other boats were engaged in a heated argument and did not notice. Stuart folded his arms and watched them with a resigned nonchalance.

"Hello, who's that?" whispered Matt tentatively.

"This is Inspector Flo Macrury. Is that you Stuart?" Her tone was gentle and reassuring.

"No, it's Matt Macaulay, on Stuart's boat."

"Is he with you and the woman? Are you all OK?"

"Yes, sort of, for now."

"Can you talk?"

"Not really, it's a bit hairy here to be honest."

Matt was trying to think of the best way to summarise their predicament. It seemed too ludicrous for anyone to believe. Stuart must have been reading his thoughts.

"Just tell her to get help here now!" he muttered.

Florence must have heard him, "I'll be quick then. How close are you to the shore? Are you near Loch Eynort on the East Side?"
Matt looked at Stuart, who shrugged his shoulders and nodded.
"Sort of."
"Are there any other craft nearby?"
"Yes and they are not friendly forces."
"Understood. Can you convince the party in the other boat to come ashore? I can have help waiting for you."
"I guess I can give it a go. It's boats mind, there's two of them and they are..." The line went dead.
Stuart became aware that Ivan was looking over at him. He disconnected the call on his control panel.
"I hear you. Who are you talking to?" Demanded the Russian.
"Nobody, just thinking out loud. Look mate, I've had a thought. This is my brother's

boat; I'm not really used to it you know? I'm trying to work out how best to keep it stable out

here without running into any rocks. You do know that there are loads of rocks just under the

surface here, could wreck your boat in an instant."

From the looks on the faces of the others, they hadn't thought of this. Stuart was banking

on the fact that none of the others were natural sailors or had researched the area properly.

The Russians exchanged anxious glances, but Wally who had developed an intense dislike of

Stuart was not going to be fooled and whether right or wrong had to contradict him.

"That's rubbish, I looked at the charts; there are no rocks here."

Stuart was not going to be deterred and answered equally belligerently. "Aye, well how

often do you sail round here and how far do you think we have drifted since you first turned

up and started threatening me?" He turned to Ivan.

"Look mate, I have no problem with you looking in my wee boat, but just to be clear don't think for one moment that I would have anything to do with that wanker." He pointed fiercely at Wally. The Russians laughed, they didn't really understand the word but they clearly got the drift.

"Offer to lead them ashore," whispered Matt. "Ask how they're going to board boats out here?"

Stuart turned to the Russians, sounded more confident than he felt. "I have a suggestion that might help."

Ivan and Boris were not sure how to respond to this unexpected helpfulness. They didn't trust anyone, they conferred quickly, although they would probably have to get rid of him eventually, his local knowledge could be an asset. Boris couldn't see how he could be involved; maybe he was just in the wrong place at the wrong time. But Ivan was more suspicious, something was going on between the local boat and the Americans and he wanted to get to the bottom of it.

"Continue," Boris nodded finally.

"Well, as you can see we all are drifting," he waved around him to emphasis his point, "I'm drifting and unstable due to my creel lines still being attached. There are, as I said, hidden rocks out here. How are you going to maintain position and board anyone's boat? It's a risky business. Why don't I lead us all ashore then you can look in the boats properly on land? There's a little shingle inlet that is covered in seaweed. It's out of the way. No one's going far on the seaweed, especially while you have that gun pointed at us." He shrugged as if totally unconcerned.

"That's total crap," blurted Wally. He frowned and sounded like a small child frustrated at being dragged away from his prize.

Ivan was even more convinced that there was something more going on between the two boats. He sighed. It would have been more convenient to kill them all at sea, but now he just wanted to thwart whatever else the American was up to.

"Ok... You..." Ivan barked as Boris swung the gun ominously round towards Stuart, "lead the way. You, second." He pointed at the Americans, "and we will be behind, with both your boats in Range." He leant over and tapped the gun to make sure his meaning was clear. "How long will it take?"

"Oh, only about ten minutes," responded Stuart, already turning his boat around.

"Don't make it look too easy," hissed Matt. "We have to give Flo time to get here."

The Lady Mary started towards the shore, slowly leading the strange looking flotilla she wound her way into the mouth of the loch snuggled between the hills. They tacked a little for good effect as the other boats followed. He manoeuvred the boat awkwardly against the tide, to make the journey just that little bit more hazardous and uncomfortable for those following.

It was working; behind them the Russians were beginning to relax slightly. To them the local man seemed to have been telling the truth. They could see the small beach surrounded by woodland; it appeared secluded. Little did they know that it was one of the easier access points on the east side of Uist. The two Americans on the other hand were increasingly more frustrated. They were getting soaked. Their little boat was being tossed around in the waves and being drenched with sea spray. Despite the fact that they had been planning to dive, they were not prepared for this. Hank was concentrating on steering the vessel while Wally stood closely behind him. He had dropped the flare gun but was not helping; he was talking intently to Hank, who was not welcoming the distraction. He tried to assert his authority and barked at Wally to shut up, but to no avail. Their bickering became more furious. It was a loud and heated debate.

"I think we've got a mutiny going on behind us," Stuart called out in Gaelic as he turned the Lady Mary again. "This might just work. I just hope nobody sees me sailing like this, I'll never live it down."

"This is ridiculous!" moaned Wally as they turned again. "Just head straight to the shore... We have the smallest, fastest boat; we can get there first and deal with them then."

"With what? We're out gunned and outnumbered."

"No way, they're not working together... surely?"

"All this about him just fishing, and the Russkies looking for that woman sounds like an ambush to me. He was just keeping us there till they turned up."

"Exactly, I'm not having them steal our gold. We found it."

"If we go straight ashore, they are simply going to disable us or worse and go back and get it for themselves. This at least gives us time to think and come up with a plan," argued Hank.

"What do you suggest then?" Wally was becoming more impatient.

Hank didn't answer. He was beginning to regret this ill fated trip. He could see his whole life's work and career slipping away in front of him. This should have been so simple. He had a gut wrenching sense of impending doom. He couldn't think straight. He had never been superstitious, but cold and wet on the ocean, the memory of the chilling curse was crippling his thinking. He looked behind him. The Russians were struggling too. He hadn't paid too much attention to it at the time, but suddenly he didn't know whether to be more worried about the machine gun behind him or the wrath of a long dead ancient Chief. He shook his head, trying to clear his thoughts. He was angry at himself for ever meeting up with the historical society back home, but he couldn't blame them. It was he who told Wally of the legend when they realised they were going to be part of the exercise in Scotland eighteen months ago. He should never have gone along with the plan. But then he never really expected to find anything. Perhaps Wally was right; maybe they should just get back to the shore.

Wally's brain on the other hand was working in overtime. He was determined that he was not going to be robbed!

"You're right. There's no point in going ashore to be shot. Let's swim for it."

"Are you mad? Where to?"

"We have the gear. We came out here to dive, so let's just go," Wally insisted.

Hank realised that he wasn't asking or waiting. He was stripping off his jacket and trousers to reveal his wet suit. As he reached for an oxygen tank Hank left the controls and tried to grab him.

"Wal, wait, this is suicide..." pleaded Hank, but there was no stopping him.

The Russians seeing the activity started shouting at the Americans to stop. They drew their boat closer just in time to witness Wally flip over the side. Ivan opened fire aiming at the surface of the water. Bullets skimmed into the waves. Stuart looked round as the sound pierced the air. Hank partly to protect Wally and partly in the vain hope that if he died in combat at least in some way his honour would be saved, grabbed the wheel again. He spun the boat around, twisted the throttle and aimed straight at the Russians.

"Go, go, go!" yelled Matt but Stuart didn't need telling; he'd heard the almighty crash behind them too. The piercing, thunderous clatter of gunfire was ringing in his ears as he pulled back the throttle and aimed straight for the shore. Matt half pulled and half dragged a struggling Alex out of the cupboard.

"Hold on tight!" he yelled as the Lady Mary bucked and crashed noisily against the waves that were being churned up by the speed of the boat.

It only took a few minutes, but it was a wild few minutes. The Lady Mary shook and bounced over the swell. Stuart hung on for grim death to keep the boat straight. Below deck

Matt hung on to Alex with one arm and the side of the boat with the other; he was terrified that she would go flying or hurt herself at any moment.

Suddenly, with a spine chilling screech the small boat slammed to a halt. Stuart was hurled across the deck and landed with a sickening thud against the gunwale, ropes and fish boxes clattering down on top of him. Matt and Alex were thrown forward hard against the hatch, the remaining contents of the wheel house rattling behind them. Alex was whimpering, but Matt knew they had no time to feel sorry for themselves.

"C'mon, gotta go," he pulled her on to her feet and pushed her up onto the deck.

"Stuart boy, get up mate, we've got to move." He breathed a brief sigh of relief, happy to hear his friend groan beneath the debris.

Matt moved quickly. With Alex's help he pulled the debris off his friend and roughly pulled him upright.

"We got to move boyo. I don't know how close behind us those buggers are; we got to get out of here."

"I know, I know." Stuart closed his eyes and concentrated for a moment. "Just a wee bit winded, that's all. I take it we've made the shore?" he quipped, pulling himself to his feet. Joking always helped.

"Aye, but we've no time to be admiring the view."

They scrambled over the side and into the water. It was a sudden shock, cold and salty stinging against their skin, the acrid smell of smoke was on the wind. They could hear shouting, but none of them dare look behind. Stuart was relieved to find that it was not very deep, it was just about chest height on him. He could see the beach looking invitingly close, despite the fact that it was covered in dark slippery kelp. He really just wanted to be on dry land.

"We could stand up you know," he called.

"No, keep low, we don't want to draw attention to ourselves." He scanned the shore ahead. It was a small shingle beach brown with a knee deep layer of kelp that grew out of the water. Further back there was a thin line of shale that led into a small forest. On the left, obscuring the path into the hills was an abandoned, weathered boat mounted on stilts. Rocky outcrops cut the bay off from the rest of the shoreline. They had them cornered.

"Keep right. Head for the trees."

Whether it was the adrenalin, the sludge or the cold, it did not take them long to reach the shore. Matt led the way up the beach. He looked around briefly then spotted an ideal position. Halfway into the woods there was a cluster of bushes on a slight rise sprouting in front of a rock. That will do, he thought. A little bit of shelter and a grandstand view. It was only when they were bedded down behind the rock that they dared to look back out to sea.

Stuart looked forlornly at the Lady Mary. It was listing pathetically in the slime, still being pounded by the waves.

"That's the last time I go fishing with you Macaulay."

"I dunno. Think we did better than some."

Matt was looking further out trying work out exactly what it was that had just happened. The two other boats were in an untidy heap, one thrown half way across the other, only they shouldn't be that way at sea. Black smoke was pouring from one of them, but Matt couldn't tell which. He squinted. He couldn't see anyone trying to fight the fire. In fact, he couldn't see anyone on board either boat at all.

"Oh shit, I think they're all in the water."

175

"Well at least the shooting's stopped."

"Should we try and help? Normally I'd be rushing in, but I'm a bit wary of that gun."

Matt considered. In his previous life Matt knew exactly what he would do... but this was Uist.

"Problem solved." Stuart pointed at the horizon. "They took their time, but the cavalry's finally here."

"Looks like they got the ground troops too," agreed Matt. They could hear shouting and the howling of a police siren in the distance, they hoped they were heading in their direction.

Two larger boats had appeared on the horizon coming into the loch; one was clearly identified as the Barra Life Boat, the other looked like a Marine Harvest well boat. He could see the company's distinctive colours. Florence must have worked quickly and pulled everyone in, thought Matt. At the other end of the beach a number of people were clambering onto the stones and jumping over the rocks as they appeared like ants from behind the abandoned boat. He could see the police uniforms of Florence Macrury and her men. There was also a number of Range staff emerging onto the beach. Frank and Carl were running onto the shingle and into the seaweed regardless of their own safety or comfort. They were followed by Bob Halifax; the Dutchmen and a couple of others at a slower pace, gingerly making their way towards the water.

Stuart began to pull himself to his feet but Matt pulled him back. "Let's just stay here for a minute. I don't want everyone to see Alex and wonder what she is doing here with us."

Stuart gave him a quizzical look but despite how cold he felt, he didn't argue.

They watched as Florence directed the rescue from the shore and the lifeboat closed on the burning boats in the water. Effort was being focussed on retrieving those in the water. Matt could see what looked like three people floundering in the water. He wondered what had happened to the fourth and to their assorted weaponry. Somebody broke away from the crowd of rescuers and headed towards the beached remains of the Lady Mary and began to climb aboard. It was Carl. Matt watched him make a sweeping search of the boat, it didn't take long. He reappeared onto the deck and started to scan the shore and the edge of the woods. It didn't take him long to see the damp footprints they had left at the other end of the beach. He stared directly at the trees. Had he seen them? Matt was willing him not to raise the alarm.

Carl turned and looked towards the rescuers, then back towards the woods. He was obviously weighing the situation up. He made up his mind. He climbed out of the boat, throwing a quick glance over his shoulder at the commotion at the water's edge; he headed slowly towards the forest following nonchalantly in their footsteps. As he got closer his footsteps quickened. He didn't know why they were hiding, but he wasn't going to blow their cover. He sat down close by on the soft pine needles slightly away from the boulder.

"You guys keeping out of the way then? I would too if I did that to Paul Steele's boat. You all OK?"

"We survived, just about. Thanks for raising the alarm. You probably saved our skins and I'm impressed with all the collateral you brought."

"That's one way of putting it. Got a bit touch and go for a while, but it was the Inspector really. She spoke to some lad in Glasgow, I think she was concentrating on getting Dr. Alex out of here. Not sure what that was about, but she got the lifeboat in, and the Marine Harvest boys to cover all eventualities and it seems she was right."

"I still need to get Alex out of here discreetly. Do you have a car parked up there?"

"Yep, no problem it's in the car park, but there are a lot of people about."

"OK Alex and I will head for the hills, we will have to double back and take the top path so as to hopefully miss them. Stuart you go back down there with Carl and tell them how it was...don't let them get away with anything, but don't let on that we were there with you. "

"But what about the Inspector, she knows," interrupted Carl.

"If she has spoken to Murdo she won't let on."

Carl and Stuart exchanged glances; they didn't really understand or quite believe their friend, but trusted him enough to go along with his plan.

"Hey, I'm more than ready to have another conversation with them Americans," answered Stuart, not letting them get away with any bull."

"It was the Americans? Bloody hell! Did you find out who the person they were talking to was?" Carl was shocked. "I thought it was the Russians".

"What other person?" Asked Stuart.

"They had an accomplice, who might still be about so watch out. Listen, we don't have time to hang around. You two have the whole story between you, Alex and I will back you up from the Glasgow end. Just give us a bit of a head start and for people not to know that Alex is with me. OK? I don't want the Russians to have the opportunity to raise the alarm about Alex."

The plan was agreed. In an unusual display of warmth Alex gave Stuart and Carl a quick hug before disappearing towards the road with Matt.

Watching his friend leave Stuart suddenly felt very tired. His experience of the last few hours had shown him the type of danger Matt was in and he was worried for his friend, but he was determined to see this through.

He staggered slightly as he turned to follow Carl. The wind chilled his wet clothes and he ached all over as he squelched his way back along the beach. He pulled his phone out of his pocket and he watched as water poured out of the case; it was as wet as he was. He wanted to go home and get dry but he had a score to settle. The younger man put his arm around his shoulder to support him.

"Help, Help." Carl waved his free arm in the air. "I've got Stuart. We need help here."

"I'm not that bad mate." Sighed Stuart, although he didn't really feel it.

"Just getting us in on the party."

Florence rushed up the beach to meet them. "Let's get you out of here into the warm and dry, then we can talk."
"No, I have a few words to say to them coming ashore." He was adamant.
"It's all right honestly. The fish farm boat has picked up the survivors of your

waterborne pile up. The medics are dealing with them. Sounds as if that American Officer,

Hank is it, seems to have been some sort of hero, or at least he claims trying to save his

colleague and the Russians. He is a bit vague though about what he was doing there. Bob

Halifax is talking with him now."

"I think we should join that conversation," suggested Stuart.

"Aye, too right," agreed Carl.

Florence looked from one to the other. "Is Matt going to join us?"

"No," was the reply in unison. She was taken aback with the immediacy of the response,

especially when she knew that Matt had been there, but she had dealt with Matt Macaulay

before. She understood from Murdo that he had another agenda. She would go with the flow.

"OK, they are talking by the first aid station where they are bringing people ashore. They

have set up some tarpaulins as an emergency point by the old boat out of the wind as a triage

station before taking people back to the road. Let's get over there, get you warmed up and

see what is going on."

As they approached the boat they could see one man sat on what looked like a camping

chair. He was wrapped in a silvery survival blanket being attended to by a paramedic, with

Bob Halifax hovering beside him. Bob came forward to meet them, offering Stuart a blanket.

Stuart ignored him, but Carl took the blanket, unfurled it and wrapped it around Stuart's

shoulders. Undeterred, Bob came forward as if to assist, closing in to have a quiet word.

"I am very glad to see that you are Ok son, was it only you on your boat?"

Stuart still ignored him. Oblivious, Bob continued.

"The Police are managing this rescue, but as there is ... how can I put it? A military involvement here, I am taking the lead as the Senior British officer."

"Where is everyone else? Shouldn't Mike or Skip be in charge?" Asked Carl.

"They have escorted the Russian casualties to hospital with the Police. I think Frank is still helping with the search for the other American along the beach, we fear that he is more seriously injured. We can do a proper debrief later, but right now, I want to keep things simple while we are in public, so would be happy if you can go along with Hank's version of events. Don't want any spurious stories getting into the papers now do we?"

Stuart glared at him with icy contempt.

"Spurious? I'm not in the effing military and I don't call attempted murder, environmental carnage and frigging piracy spurious!"

"Exactly, exactly," Bob was nervously trying to placate him. "You were lucky that Hank was there to save you!"

"Really? This is going to be interesting, let's hear what he has to say shall we?" Stuart shrugged off his assistants and with new found energy strode towards the ambulance. As he got close, Hank rose to his feet. He reached out to Stuart and attempted to hug him. He appeared overcome with emotion.

"Oh son, I am so glad to see you alive. I was so scared we'd lost you." He sobbed. Stuart shrugged him off. Bob put a reassuring hand on his shoulder. He was the only one who seemed to believe the theatrics. Carl and Florence looked on without comment.

"Well, that is what happens when you point guns at people eh!" Stuart replied stonily.

"We didn't fire at you. It was the Russians. They opened fire which kind of unbalanced their boat, we knew we had to stop them, so did the only thing we could, we turned our craft and rammed them. That made their boat capsize, but not before they fired again. They hit Wally, he's fallen into the water. I don't know if he is alive or dead. They are looking for him. He's died saving you and your passengers." With that he collapsed sobbing back onto the tailgate of the ambulance. Bob consoled him. The others remained unmoved.

"That's all as maybe, I didn't see," conceded Stuart. "But it was you and your pal who were threatening me. What were you doing there? Looked like you wanted me out of the way so that you could go diving. Aye, down to the wreck that you and your mates killed all those poor wee fish to find. You're not heroes, just old fashioned thieving scum."

"I explained that, it was Range business," muttered Hank. Bob nodded knowingly.

"What the same Range business that had you driving the Russian Sub around last night and bragging to your pals about what you had found at that very spot," interrupted Carl. "I saw ye. You didnae give a shit about the beasties dying because of you. Just greedy to steal the gold." The young man was shaking with anger. Florence stepped forward putting her hand on his shoulder.

"Not now son. Don't worry. This will all be investigated, military involvement or not. She signalled to the paramedics and a couple of nearby policemen. "I think we should start getting you people off to the hospital... with a police escort." She turned to Bob. "I would be grateful if you do not attempt to leave Uist. I will need to understand everyone's involvement."

Bob was about to protest, but was cut short by shouting from further down the shore. It was Frank who was waist deep in the water, reaching out to something floating just out of reach. "Help, help... Over here. I've found him!"

Frank was lifting what appeared to be a dark lifeless bundle on to the rocks. Everyone rushed to help him. He stood, still fully dressed, shivering in the water, watching as the paramedics carried the sopping body and laid it carefully on the ground. Together with a medic from the lifeboat they tried their best to save him, but he died, there, by the waterside.

Frank remained in the water as they carried Wally's body away. He was soaked and covered in the dead man's blood. He was staring out to sea. Stuart crouched down beside him on the rock. He held out his hand to help the older man ashore.

"C'mon, we should both get dry," he urged, but Frank did not move.

Carl brought over a survival blanket and wrapped it round the older man's shoulders as he clambered out of the water. He looked up and smiled weakly in gratitude. He turned back to the sea.

"Look, it's beautiful out there, what makes people want to... I don't know, I can't even find the words. It's all so pointless..."

They helped him to his feet and started to make their way back to the road in silence. There were still several emergency vehicles parked at the side of the road. People were waiting as the transport was being organised.

Frank looked around. "Where's your car?" he asked Carl.

"Matt took it. To get Doctor Alex away." Carl replied quietly.

"Ah yes, I should have thought. Are they OK?"

"Well, they were in one piece the last time I saw them. Which is more than he will be when Paul sees his boat." Stuart was trying to lighten the moment, but it didn't work.

"That's not funny. Do either of you know where they went? They could still be in danger. We don't know if Boris and Ivan have any other friends on the island."

"He didn't seem worried." Carl tried to assure him.

"Yes that's just it though. He never does."

Stuart wasn't listening, he moved to one side watching as the police and medics were shepherding the walking wounded into the remaining police cars and ambulances.

"It's not just the Russians' friends we should worry about though, is it?"

The other two turned to see who he was looking at.

"Who is the yank talking to? He definitely isn't offering hic condolences. Isn't it the guy who was just bugging you? I'm sure he was writing something down a minute ago."

"That's Bob," replied Carl. "So much for an on Range investigation."

"I think I will have a word with Florence", muttered Frank. He sauntered over to the police woman and spoke quietly into her ear. She listened intently and nodded. "Leave it to me".

As Frank rejoined Carl and Stuart they watched as the Inspector approached Bob Halifax. She quietly, but firmly offered him a lift in her car. He demurred at first, but the expression on his face changed as he realised that he didn't have an option.

~~~~~~~~~~~~~~~~~~~~~~~~~~~~~~

Chapter Seventeen: Goodbyes

Away from all the commotion Matt and Alex made their way through the woods. The bed of soft pine needles felt warm and reassuring underfoot and the trees provided shelter from the wind and commotion; a different world from the one they had just left. Matt explained that the woods bordered a maze of tracks that that linked around the Ben Mhor foot hills. Built to give visitors access to the area, they provided a variety of routes to get them back to Carl's car without being seen. As they left the wood the winding path was just wide enough for one person. They were sheltered by shoulder high hedgerows so could not be easily seen, even so, they circled around to avoid the would- be rescuers who were heading straight to the beach. As they approached the car park there was a line of four by fours parked with a couple of emergency vehicles blocking the main track. Matt was amazed how they had actually got so many vehicles down there as it was a narrow access road to the beauty spot. A policeman stood by his car with its door open, he was probably left on guard. He had his back to them and was talking avidly on the phone, so didn't see them as they trotted silently by.

Matt quickly spotted Carl's car. It was quite close by with space to turn back onto the track. Keeping low, they ran up behind it. As Matt expected the doors were unlocked, they slipped in quietly. The Policeman still had his back to them and the keys were in the ignition.

"This will do us." Matt started the engine, he was watching the Policeman. Whoever was talking to him had the copper's full attention and he didn't notice them.

Alex was shivering, her hair was plastered to her head, her face was patched with sea weed and grass, her arms were crossed with her hands tucked tightly under her armpits in a vain attempt to warm them up. Her teeth began to chatter loudly. Matt turned the heating on.

"It will warm up in a minute," he assured her. Alex nodded in response and gave him a weak smile.

"Last leg now. We'll find us some dry clothes and have you off here in no time OK?"

Matt had expected some sort of complaint about further delays but instead there was just a quiet, "Thank you."

He turned the car around. As they started to pull away, the police man glanced over his shoulder. Matt gave him a cheery wave. The Policeman returned the gesture and turned back to the excitement, it was far more interesting than one of the Range guys heading off.

Matt wasn't wasting any time, he drove the car quickly on the single track twisting road as they bounced and rattled across the hillside, Matt was worried that the little car would not make it, but once on the main road he gratefully headed for Bornish his exhaust apparently intact. They could get changed and he could contact Murdo from there. Nobody had associated Alex with him and he doubted very much if anyone was seriously chasing her on land as yet, the Russians thought she was on the Americans' boat, which gave him an idea.

He explained this to Alex as they drove along, again expecting some argument. Instead she just agreed meekly. He looked over at her. She was staring out of the window. She wasn't exactly smiling; the only word he could think of to describe her expression was enigmatic. Which was odd. "Are you OK?"

"Yes I am fine, very fine. You were right. It feels good to know that those two are learning how to swim with the help of your police, while I am on my way to safety to stop them and the people they work for. I feel hope for the first time in a long while."

Matt was surprised. Perhaps she was in shock. "We need to keep it that way. I will be introducing you to my employer. He works for the Scottish Government; he will look after you in Glasgow." The thought of Murdo looking after anyone sounded fraught to Matt, but he didn't know how else to put it. He was sure Murdo could be nice if he needed to be.

They turned at the Bornish junction and followed the single track road that wound between field and loch into the Township. Finally, Alex watched as Matt pulled off onto a short gravel track that led up to a two story box house with an old stone shed set back slightly to the left of it. They rattled across a cattle grid. Matt could only see his mother's car parked out front, but he wasn't taking any risks at this stage, he drove round the house and pulled up behind the shed so that the car was out of sight from the road.

The scent of the peat fire wafting gently from the chimney was warming in itself as they approached the back door. Matt knew it would be unlocked and he stepped quietly into the utility room that housed the washer and dryer, a large chest freezer, bags of dog food and assorted junk. Their arrival was announced by the dog barking in the kitchen, his mum would not be far. Out of habit Matt slipped off his wet shoes, Alex followed his example.

"Hi Mam, I'm home," he called into the house. "I have someone with me."

"Yes, Murdo said you might." His mother replied as they entered the kitchen. She was putting the kettle on in anticipation of serving tea.

"You've been talking to Murdo?"

"Hello my dear, my name is Seonag," she addressed Alex. She looked from one to the other. "*Che, Che*, You two are soaked. Matt get some towels from the airing cupboard." She fussed. "The world and his wife have been looking for you this morning."

"This is Alex mam; do you think it will be OK if she borrows some of the girls' spare clothes. They've left bits and pieces in their rooms haven't they? What did Murdo say? Who else is looking for me?"

"He will be here in a bit and yes of course you can have dry clothes Ma tha. I expect you will want to be sorted before he arrives. Show her to the bathroom and I will look something out."

Alex was having difficulty following the conversation, but was happy with the opportunity to dry off and warm up, plus what sounded like the arrival of Matt's contact. She wondered how much Matt's mother knew.

186

While Alex showered Matt changed quickly and re-joined his mother in the kitchen.

"I am going to have to keep a whole spare wardrobe if you are going to keep bringing home waifs and strays Matt. This is becoming a habit."

Matt knew that she didn't mind really. "I thought you already had one, mam," he retorted. "Who else has been looking for me?"

"Well, that Murdo rang twice; he said he had landed at the airport and would drive here. Were you expecting him?" She didn't wait for a reply. "Then Sarah rang. Said it was something about a poem and she would ring back. After that Kate called, she said to call her, but didn't say why. Said it was probably nothing but call her anyway. Which is odd but you know what she is like, probably wants help with one of her stories." Seonag paused for breath. Matt felt that uneasy tingle at the back of his neck. What did Kate want? She should be at the Spar store with Marieke. He was about to tell his mother that he would ring her back, but his mother hadn't finished yet.

"I've been having some weird calls too."

"What?"

"Yes, it has rung three times, but each time I have answered there has been nobody there. It's not Iona, I checked." I was beginning to get concerned. Next time it rings; will you answer it? I was worried it was you, you know. I take it that you and her had something to do with the goings on at Stuley this morning?"

"I can't talk about this morning mam, but we are fine and of course I'll answer the phone. It's probably nothing. I'll just give Kate a quick ring..."

But he didn't get the chance. The dog was barking at the sound of a car coming over the cattle grid. He looked out of the front window. Murdo had arrived.

Matt wasn't sure what sort of reception he would get from Murdo; he had after all disobeyed the man's orders again. But he was pleasantly surprised, the normally dour

Glaswegian was all smiles, greeting Seonag with a hug and shaking her hand warmly. Seonag had met Murdo previously when Matt had brought him back wet and bedraggled after a mishap on the hillside. She credited Murdo for helping Matt get back on his feet and giving him an interest in life again as well as a job.

"I'll put the kettle on, then go up and see how the lassie is doing Ok?"

"Thanks Seonag," nodded Murdo "Be great if you could give us a few minutes before she comes down."

Murdo made himself at home, pulling a chair out from the kitchen table to sit on as Seonag headed up the stairs.

"Is she alright?" Murdo asked quietly.

"Yes, she's fine." Matt replied. "Look, about the fish and the treasure stuff, I just couldn't ignore it." Matt needed to get it off his chest.

"Yes, yes of course. I understand, worked out well too. I didn't want us starting an international incident, but if the Americans and Russians want one of their own that is up to them as far as I am concerned. A lot of noise about treasure, while the good Doctor slips away quietly will suit us just fine. Nobody has missed her yet have they?"

"No. about that, I did have a thought." Matt sat down opposite Murdo, feeling more relaxed now that he knew he wasn't in trouble. "Why don't we declare her lost at sea... don't need to find a body, just maybe a phone or some clothing... you know what the currents are like out there? Well perhaps you don't, but you get my drift."

"Let me think about it. I was thinking of requesting that young lad, Carl is it? To work on an investigation team, to give us the details of what went on. He has the details of the pollution and indeed the potential wreck with all its treasure hasn't he?" Murdo thought he could see a hint of disappointment on Matt's face. Perhaps he had wanted to follow it through himself. Normally he would have allowed Matt to escort Alex away, but he would have to get to that later. "Thanks to Florence we have all of them in custody and well, something has come up, I have another job for you."

"Yes, Carl would be fine, I think he will like that and it will give some time for things to settle on the Range. He has all the information first hand, so would be a good choice."

"That's settled. Now we just have to get this lassie out of here. She is going on the Air Ambulance. I have booked an ambulance to pick her up from here, which will drive her straight onto the plane without anyone seeing her. I have spoken with the medical people, it's all arranged, she will be dressed as a medic accompanying the body."

At that point Seonag and Alex came back into the room.

Just as Murdo began to introduce himself the phone rang. Seonag picked it up, but Matt indicated to her that he would answer it. He stepped back out into the utility room.

"Good afternoon, Macauley house," he answered formally.

"Och Matt it's you. You've gone and done it haven't you, you've found the treasure!"

It was Sarah, her voice booming down the line sounding very excited.

"Hi Sarah, look, thanks for your help, I can't say anything about that and am in the middle of things right now. I'll call you later."

"No, no listen, I guess you can't say, but I heard about all the commotion at Stuley and two and two do sometimes make five. But seriously, with my work hat on, if there is something of cultural significance who should I direct my questions at?"

"Well, I'm not saying anything, but if I were you, I'd ring Carl MacPhee tomorrow."

"Ah that's lovely."

"Lovely?" Had she finally lost it?

"Sorry yes, I found the full story about the Irish warlord. He wrote more about his daughter's death. He wrote a prayer in which he asked for a guardian angel, a young warrior to look after

Uist and his daughter. Perhaps his wish has been granted. Anyway, I'll catch up with Carl.
Leave you to it, bye, bye now."

Matt shook his head as he came off the phone, perhaps it was better leaving Carl to follow up, the woman was a whirlwind and there would be more like her when the news got out.

As he went back into the kitchen, Matt could see an Ambulance pulling up at the front of the house. That was quick, he thought. Murdo and Alex were both standing, facing each other. Murdo's hands were placed protectively on the woman's slight shoulders. He was talking quietly and she was nodding.

"OK then, let's go." He looked out the window. "Your transport is here."

Murdo took the scientist by the shoulders and gently moved her towards the front door. Alex turned to Matt.

"Thank you," she mouthed as she disappeared from sight.

Matt sat wearily at the kitchen table; he still had the phone in his hand. "I think I need something stronger than tea now mam."

"No, we're going to have that cup of tea first. I have boiled this kettle so many times since you came in and we haven't had a drink yet. You phone Kate while I'm doing it. While we have a moment." His sister's number was preloaded into the phone. It rang quickly; then just as quickly went to voicemail. "Hi, it's me. I believe you were looking for me. Give me a call back at mam's." He hung up after leaving the message. His mother brought a plate of biscuits and three mugs over to the table and sat next to him.

"Why have you poured three cups mum?" He couldn't decide which one of them had lost the plot. He was definitely getting overtired now.

"One's for Murdo. He'll be back in a minute, didn't he tell you?"

190

"No," muttered Matt. "He didn't." It was most odd that Murdo hadn't gone with Alex. Perhaps there wasn't room. He hoped that his boss didn't want a debrief right now. He was also worried about what else Murdo had to tell him.

They had almost finished their tea by the time Murdo re-joined them. He sat down and drank from his mug enthusiastically.

"That will be cold," commented Seonag.

"Its fine." Murdo thanked her. "Just the way I like it."

"That didn't take long. I thought you would have been going with her." Matt was straight to the point as was his way.

Murdo nodded "There was limited space on the plane. She will be less conspicuous by herself and..." He paused, "I need to talk with you." He finished the last of his tea. To Matt he was taking an age. What was he putting off saying? He was mentally urging Murdo to get on with it.

"The thing is, we have lost contact with Marieke. She is not at the flat. We were keeping an eye as you know; upped surveillance when you mentioned the car, but it is gone and so is she. I am not assuming she is in any danger yet. There is no evidence of that; she may have just lost her nerve. Did she say anything to you?"

"Did anyone look inside her flat?"

"Yes, there are no signs of a break in or struggle, in fact it looks like at least some of her and the boy's clothes are missing, almost as if they have gone on a short break or something."

"Ah," Matt smiled. "Maybe I should have said, but I was wrapped up here. Kate was thinking of inviting them to spend a few days with her at Glenmore Centre in Aviemore. I haven't spoken with Kate but I think she asked her."

Murdo visibly relaxed too. "That's OK then. It is down to her to tell us if she is going anywhere, she knows that, but I'll just have to verify that then stand people down." He tried to use his mobile but had no signal.

"Do you want to use our phone?" offered Seonag. But before he could answer, it rang again.

Forgetting her previous reluctance Seonag got up and answered.

"Ah Kate, we are just talking about you. How is Aviemore?" She listened for a moment, then sat down. "You'd better speak to your brother." She looked worried as she passed the phone to her son.

After briefly saying hello, Matt simply listened without comment to what his sister was telling him. Murdo and Seonag could only hear the echo of her voice as she spoke, but from the expression on Matt's face they knew it was not good.

"What day was that?" was his only interruption.

"OK, Murdo's here, so I'll let him know. I'll call you later." He hung up.

Matt closed his eyes and took a deep breath. He tried to gain perspective, but even that was bad.

"Well?" prompted Murdo.

Matt had to concentrate just to talk calmly.

"Kate invited Marieke to Glenmore earlier in the week. She initially said no because she wanted to get Kazik into a routine and had things to do. Then she rang her back the day before yesterday and asked if she could change her mind. Said that Kazik was unsettled again and she was fed up with looking over her shoulder. They arranged to meet yesterday, but when Kate got there she wasn't in. Kate hung around, but she didn't show and she isn't answering her mobile. Kate went back today; she still isn't there."

"If I can use your phone, I'll make some calls. Get an alert out on that car and get port and airport checks. She may still have just got spooked and gone into hiding though; she is a resourceful girl. Let's not jump to conclusions." He was trying to sound reassuring, but the worry was written all over his face too.

Matt was about to hand him the phone when it rang again.

"Oh for goodness sake!" Muttered Matt.

"Hello."

There was no response, just a crackly silence then the line went dead.

"That's just what happened earlier," Seonag told them.

Matt looked at the phone for a second, then pressed the "last caller" button. An automated voice repeated the number of the last incoming call.

"I didn't think of that," said Seonag. "Do you know who it is?"

"It's Marieke," replied Matt. "I'll call her back."

After three rings it was answered.

"Marieke?"

He was sure he could hear light, fast breathing. But there was no reply.

A thought struck him. "Kazik, is that you? This is Matt. Where are you?"

The breathing quickened further.

"Matt? Help! Matt Help! The mans got us!"

"Be brave wee man. You tell mummy that I'm coming to get you. It will be OK."

Matt didn't know how much of that Kazik had heard as the line went dead.

*****

.

18550395R00113

Printed in Great Britain
by Amazon